MW01712378

In Rod We Trust

A collection of stories
inspired by Rod Serling's
The Twilight Zone
television series

Tom Sawyer

BLACK BED SHEET

In Rod We Trust
A Black Bed Sheet/Diverse Media Book
May 2020

ISBN-10: 1-946874-17-5
ISBN-13: 978-1-946874-17-7

In Rod We Trust

Jace,
Best Wishes!
Tom Sawyer

A Black Bed Sheet/Diverse Media Book
Antelope, CA

Also by Tom Sawyer

The Lighthouse

Fire Sale

The Sisigwad Papers

The Last Big Hit

Shadows in the Dark

Dark Harbors

From Paradise to Hell

White Out

The Thing from Uranus

Dedicated to my Dad

Thanks for giving a love and appreciation of history, reading, movies and great television series and playing baseball in the backyard with us as kids.

STORIES

Acknowledgements

Like I said before, no man is an island. I am not, nor do I pretend to be. I may have written the story, but I had lots of help in one way or another along the way. Besides, I have been too blessed in my life, by too many people for that to be so.

So, first and foremost, I once again, thank God. I thank Him for the people He has blessed me with in my life and for giving me some writing ability that in turn became a passion and sometimes an obsession. I owe everything to God, for He has blessed me.

Next, my wife Colleen. Her honesty and love has been the best thing in my life for over thirty-seven years. I know when she likes one of my stories that it is good, and most people will like it. She is my most honest critic and I do appreciate that. I am blessed to have her in my life. She is the best.

My kids, Jonathon and his wife Megan, Kathleen and her husband Ryan and Elizabeth and her fiancé Aaron, whose love and support, like Colleen's, have both sustained and motivated me to keep at it. They all are one of the best parts of my life as well. Jonathon is my first editor. All the stories go through him and he is a writer in his own right too. Elizabeth is the news and feature writer that I could never be. Kathleen takes after Mom and is another artist in the family.

My brother Tim, who is no longer with us. Somehow, when I hit a dry spell while writing, I know his spirit is around to help get me through the dry spells and writer's block I go through at times.

My in-laws, Nancy and Jerry Wern, and their love, encouragement and support throughout the years and that I had it in me to do this.

My mother, Myrna, for warping my young mind enough to like horror, sci-fi and other suspenseful things. She gets both the blame and the credit, depending on how one looks at things. I still regret that I did not do this when she was still alive.

My dad and stepmother Gene and Joan Sawyer.

Perhaps some of my biggest fans and supporters of my writing are my sister-in-law and her family, Sheryl, Jack and Brent Green. Their encouragement has meant a lot through the years.

Coming from a large family, I have plenty of aunts, uncles and cousins who I have been very fortunate to be in the same family with. Their love, support and encouragement has been great. Sadly, when it comes to some aunts and uncles, they are no longer with us, but shall remain in my heart and memories for as long as I shall live. I would list them all, but that might take another book. So, I hope a blanket thank you will suffice to all of my aunts, uncles and cousins.

I have to also thank all of my friends from all the different aspects of my life. The gang from back in the Stone Age days of high school, the ones at work and my writing friends are like an extra family. Their support has been great. I am fortunate that they, like my family, are large in number. So, a lifelong and special thanks to Mike Cavin, Pat Mueller, Tim Hudson, Mary Makrias, John Richter, Jerry Kitchen, and the rest of the gang who have been too numerous to mention but loved just the same.

There is also my former Beaumont hospital work family for about 20 years. Ken Davis, Dave Brush, Glen Nelson, Ken Nelson, Brian Bierley, Dave Harvey, and the rest who have been supportive and encouraging in my dream.

I also have to squeeze in my writing mentors of Al Nahajewski, Richard Lech, Catherine Lobb and Anita Lienert. Without their encouragement and teaching I probably wouldn't have been able to do the things I have accomplished so far. They have all been instrumental in my writing.

Catherine Lobb was the catalyst that really got me started and introduced me to Al and Rich.

Thank you, Kennedy's Irish Pub for also helping me through my writer's block at times too. Your liquid inspiration seems to be the ticket at times when I am really stuck when it comes to writing. The staff is second to none and I greatly appreciate them.

Next there are some people that I used to work with that I think of as friends, who like reading my stuff and give me a kind of test market. A big heartfelt thanks goes out to Mary Fronczak, and Kay Ashby Suma. Your input and critiques are very appreciated, and I cannot thank you enough.

I would also like to thank my writing friends, especially Adam and Jennifer Gifford for their advice, help, critiques and most of all their friendship throughout the years.

To anyone that I might have overlooked, I sincerely apologize and thank you all as well.

I would like to thank so many of you that are willing to take a chance on me and purchasing my books. I hope that I continue to be an entertaining writer for you. That is my most important job as far as I am concerned. I sincerely appreciate you all.

Last but not least by any means and very importantly, is legendary actress and great lady, Dee Wallace, who listened to me tell her about some of the stories I was writing for this book while we were at Motor City Nightmares Convention in April of 2019. Dee said she loved the idea and wanted a copy, and that I had better get to writing because she wanted a copy by next year's convention. Thanks for lighting a fire under me, Dee. Much appreciated.

Thanks, everybody, for your help and giving me the opportunity to entertain you. It is both an honor and a privilege that I take very seriously. Much peace, love, joy and happiness to you and yours.

I hope you enjoy the book. God bless you all!

Foreword

These thirteen stories are my personal tribute and homage to the late, great Rod Serling and his seminal show *The Twilight Zone*.

These stories vary from fantasy to the fanciful, from horror to the horrific, with excursions into the magical, the unbelievable and the whimsical and even a side trip into science fiction.

As a tribute to Rod Serling and his timeless and unforgettable show, I tried to make these stories as varied and entertaining as *The Twilight Zone* and even *Night Gallery* was.

There is no way that I consider myself anywhere close to the caliber of Mr. Serling. He was an unbelievable writer that has remained unsurpassed to this day. He was that great, and my greatest influence on me wanting to be a writer.

I knew from an early age at the first sound of the opening musical introduction to *The Twilight Zone* that we were in for something extraordinary. There was a different treat with each episode. I was hooked immediately. Since then I always wanted to write stories like that.

The stories were powerful. Especially when it came to right and wrong, prejudice and humanity, love and hatred. They have remained so even with the passage of time. *The Twilight Zone* is a legendary show because it is as relevant today as it was then.

Some of my favorite episodes were *Two, The Masks, Death's Head Revisited, The Obsolete Man, The Passersby, The Changing of the Guard, A Quality of Mercy, The Trade-Ins, He's Alive* and *On Thursday We Leave for Home.*

I think his closing monologue to his stories *Death's Head Revisited, The Obsolete Man*, and *In Praise of Pip* are some of his finest, most memorable and most haunting writing to me. The stories themselves are truly great as well. I hope I am able to one day write as well as that. I don't think anyone really can, because he was an original, but one can dream.

In high school, I began writing for a local newspaper covering primarily girls' sports and features. This was a great training ground for me. It taught me that when writing fiction that I needed to grab a reader early, much like Rod Serling's opening monologue hooked us into each show.

In 2000 I published my first book. A short time later I wrote my first *Twilight Zone*-inspired story, *The Beggar and the Devil.*

Since then, I have written a few others. They have been sprinkled throughout my other books here and there. I decided to put them all here in my tribute to Rod Serling. It is my thank you and eternal gratitude that first inspired me to write and for my all-time favorite television show.

I just hope that these stories are viewed as a worthy tribute to such a great and legendary writer. So, thank you Mr. Serling for your influence and unforgettable stories.

That being said, I have submitted for your approval and entertainment pleasure these stories.

So, without further ado, here are my stories.

From one Zoner to another.

In Rod We Trust.

The Beggar & the Devil

The beggar sat on the park bench exhausted. He momentarily closed his eyes to rest as a cool late afternoon autumn breeze blew against his face. He had just eluded a shopkeeper and his sons after stealing some Reisling Wine and fine cheese. Somehow, even in his current condition, he had gotten away. He'd eluded his pursuers through his superior knowledge of back streets and alleyways. For the moment, he was safe.

Now, he just sat there, breathing hard and sweating. His heart continued to pound. He coughed and hacked from all of the years of smoking and drinking. He was too tired to enjoy the fruits of his labor. He was just another beggar, too tired to really drink and eat at the moment.

In another life, years earlier, he was known as Alfred Hummell. Promising artist, poet, designer and political activist. Most of all, dreamer.

Once destined for greatness.

Abject failure.

Now, all he was, was a tired old beggar. A tramp. Someone who lived on the scraps and garbage of society. A dirty man in worn out clothes and a dirty, rumpled gray overcoat. Nameless, but for the title of *Beggar.*

He closed his eyes to rest and enjoy a peaceful moment. "There he is!" came a shout.

He opened his eyes only to see that the shopkeeper and his sons had found him. Before he could get up to run, they were on him. He stood up and tried to run away, but it was too late. The two sons grabbed him and started to pummel him unmercifully.

"Dirty Beggar!" the shopkeeper yelled as he grabbed the cheese out of his hands and then kicked him in the groin.

"We will show you what happens to people who steal fine wine!" said one of the shopkeeper's sons.

The beggar dropped the bottle of wine onto the ground, where it hit a rock and shattered, splashing wine all over the ground and the men. The shopkeeper's sons continued to pound him as he fell to the ground. As they continued their savage beating, the shopkeeper turned to see two large black dogs, with fierce red eyes and sharp teeth quietly approach.

They were growling and drooling as if rabid and stalking their prey.

The two men stopped their beating when they finally noticed the dogs themselves. Like their father, they turned to watch the two dog's approach.

"Run!" yelled the shopkeeper, as all three men then turned to run away, with the large dogs rapidly in pursuit.

The beggar was on the ground semi-conscious, but he could still hear the men's screams of terror and pain as the beasts tore into them. He laid there for a few minutes, coughing and gasping, as his cuts bled freely. This had been the story of his whole life. His lot in life had always been somebody else's fault, not his own. It was always somebody else that was trying to keep him down.

He knew he was better than this.

He was just never given the opportunity to show how good he was. All he needed was the right circumstances to do it.

He sensed somebody nearby. At first, he thought it might be the authorities or the shopkeeper and his sons returning. He looked up through his swollen and dazed eyes to only see a blur. He thought he was looking at some kind of reptilian beast's head with horns and jagged fangs. Then, as the beggar managed to focus more clearly through his swollen eyes, he realized that he was looking at an immaculately dressed, almost regally handsome gentlemen.

He eyed the stranger warily.

"Alfred Hummell, I presume?" the stranger said, more as a statement than a question, with a wicked smile. "It is a pleasure to finally meet you."

"Who are you?" the beggar asked as he struggled to get up off the ground.

"My name is not important right now," the stranger said, with an almost sinister grin. "But, Mr. Hummell, please allow me to introduce myself, I am a man of wealth and taste. I am, believe it or not, a friend and a potential benefactor."

"I have no friends," the beggar snapped as he finally managed to get up on his feet.

The stranger helped him back over to the park bench. He noticed that the stranger felt hot, yet clammy and somehow different. He also noticed the stranger gave off a particular odor that he could not place either. A kind of burning smell.

"Oh, but you do," replied the stranger. "Mr. Wittenburg and his sons almost caused you grave bodily harm over that petty larceny you perpetrated. That would have been such a shame. Especially, now."

"Damn Jews," he muttered, spitting out the words as if they tasted bad. "I hate them."

"Well, Mr. Hummell, they will be dealt with," the stranger said. Just then, the two large dogs returned. Their red eyes glowed and blood dripped from their mouths. Each one had what looked like a human arm bone in their mouths. They both stood almost at attention as if on review. He thought that they appeared almost unreal or otherworldly. They were like other large hunting dogs, but something about them was different. A strange, sulfuric smell emanated from them.

"Very good Phobos," the stranger said, gleefully as he rubbed the first dogs head. "Very good Deimos. Good job my pets. Return home."

The two large dogs turned and walked away, disappearing into the failing light of the late afternoon.

"I know about you, Mr. Hummell," the stranger continued as he sat down beside the beggar. "You are a man of under-appreciated and unique talents. You are my kind of man."

He was still wary but was now intrigued by the stranger and his knowledge of him. "So, what do you want with me?" he asked.

"I would like to be your generous benefactor, Mr. Hummell," the stranger answered.

Alfred Hummell died a long time ago," he replied, as he gently rubbed his wounds. "I am no longer that man. I am no longer worth being a benefactor to."

"Not getting into that art school pretty much destroyed you," the stranger said matter-of-factly. "Not really achieving in secondary school didn't help. Plus, bad business decisions. But, art school really was what hurt you. It was your dream. That may have started your downward trend, Mr. Hummell. Fortunately, for you I see a deep dark desire that still burns within you."

"How do you know this?" he asked, looking at the stranger.

For the first time he looked at the stranger in the face. He noticed that his eyes had no color. The irises were black. He could see that they were lifeless.

"I see it in your eyes," the stranger replied. "The eyes

truly are the window to the soul, you know. Yours still burn with a desire for some kind of manifest destiny. A burning desire for an indescribable kind of revenge."

The beggar rubbed his swollen eyes gently. "I still dream," he said. "I still dream big. I want to prove all of my detractors so very wrong. I want to show them. I want to show them all. I want to show the whole world. I still dream."

"Well, Mr. Hummell, I can help you," the stranger said. "What is it you crave most? What is it, you most desire in life? What do you need most for your very existence? Not to just exist, but to really, really live! What are you most passionate for? What is your aphrodisiac?"

The beggar leaned his head back and thought for a few minutes. "What I really desire," he said softly. "Hmmm." He then leaned forward. "I don't know if you can give me that. It isn't really something you can grasp with your hands."

"You would be surprised with what I can give you, Mr. Hummell," the stranger said. "I too, have some unique talents and powers."

"Power," the beggar said. "That is what I crave most. Power. Power. Prestige. Infamy. Notoriety. I want the world to know who I am. I want to be able to damn all those who would not give me a chance. I want to make them quake in their boots. Especially the Wittenburgs of the world. Them and others who have kept me from what I have deserved to have in my life. That's what I want. I want to discard and reject women, like the whores they are. As if they were rubbish. Like the ones who rejected me. That kind of power. Power and control. Control over lives like others had over my life for all of these years. I want power and greatness. That which cannot be forgotten. That which cannot be denied."

"To be God-like amongst the people?" the stranger

asked, already knowing the answer.

"Exactly!" the beggar exclaimed proudly, with glee as he stood, in spite of his injuries. "I want all of that and more. I once wanted to be a great artist and writer. Great enough to turn heads of royalty and the very wealthy. Now, I want that and more."

"I can make it so that women will kill themselves, if they cannot have you," the stranger said with a wicked smile.

"Excellent," he smiled. "Will I be an artist? An architect? A writer? A poet? A leader of some kind?"

"Mr. Hummell," the stranger said. "In your own way, you will be all that and much, much more. I can almost guarantee it."

"Excellent," he said with an equally wicked grin. "I would give my soul to have all that you speak of."

"I know, Mr. Hummell," said the stranger. "That is why I would like to be your benefactor. You are perfect for what I have in mind."

"So, what is required of me?" the beggar said as he sat back down.

"Have you ever heard of soul transformation?" the stranger asked.

"No," replied the beggar.

"Well, it is a simple procedure," the stranger continued to explain. "All you have to do is find someone with the same initials and birth date as yourself."

"Oh, that's all," he said sarcastically. "There are hundreds of people in this village. How am I to find the exact one? It's impossible. So much for my dreams of power and grandeur."

"That is where I come in, Mr. Hummell," the stranger explained. "It is easier than you think. I know of a four-year-old boy on the other side of the village who shares both your initials and birth date."

"Really?"

"Yes," replied the stranger. Usually this must be done on your birthdays."

"My birthday is in April. I don't think I can make it until then. I am too injured to make it to the other side of the village anyway.

"I know," the stranger said. "But tonight is Old Hallow's Eve, thus making it a night where souls are closest to the earth and perfect for soul transformation."

"Transportation will be provided," the stranger said. "We just cannot have you missing out on this opportunity."

The stranger then whistled. Out of nowhere a black carriage with two large black horses with red eyes rode up. They were driven by an indistinguishable hooded figure with no visible face.

The stranger helped the beggar up and into the carriage. Inside the carriage was a plush and comfortable crimson red. It was something only the very wealthy or royalty could afford or even dream of riding in.

"Aaahh, yes October," said the stranger, once he was inside the carriage. "It is a lovely time for a carriage ride, would you not say, Mr. Hummell?"

"I suppose it is. At least the temperatures are pleasant this year."

"Do you realize it is Old Hallows Eve?" the stranger asked.

The beggar shook his head no. "Time is of no importance to me," he answered. "I don't even know what year it is anymore."

"I can understand that," the stranger said. "Being in the position that you are in."

"This soul transformation," the beggar said. "What is it, exactly? What do I have to do? How does it work?"

"Well, first of all, you have to touch the other

person," the stranger replied. "You have to touch the other person and recite a certain incantation three times either on the day of your births or on the holiday of Old Hallow's Eve. The power generated by the dead souls will enable the transformation. Your soul will leave your body and pass into his, while his will pass into yours. A trade of sorts. As well as, a second chance for you."

"That's all there is?"

"Well, there is a bit of a charge that will give you a bit of a shock and numb your senses," the stranger replied. "Nothing too terribly bad. You may even be unconscious for a little while.

"That's it then?"

"Yes," the stranger answered and then nodded and pointed.

The carriage driver then hit the reigns and the horses took off down the road and through the town at an incomprehensible speed. The beggar could not believe how fast they arrived at the other side of town. He saw a few people here and there, but none seemed to notice the carriage or its occupants. The beggar noticed that the horses and the carriage made no noise. It was as if they were not really there.

Instead of arriving on the other side of the village in minutes, they were there in seconds. The carriage stopped and his new friend and benefactor climbed out. The carriage then took off down the road and disappeared from sight.

"Well, we are at the house of the little boy," the stranger said. "We are actually near the back of his house. Now, you just have to wait for the boy to come out so you can do the soul transformation."

The beggar finally realized who he was talking to. "You're him, aren't you?" he asked, having trouble saying the words. "You're him. You are…are…the Devil, aren't you? You are Satan."

The stranger bowed his head slightly. "Yes, I am. In the flesh." he replied. "Also known as Lucifer, the Prince of Darkness. Lord of Flies. The Fallen Angel. Just to name a few of the titles bestowed on me throughout the ages. I actually like the Prince of Darkness best. It sounds so regal and powerful."

The beggar was stunned and moved away from the stranger he had now identified as the Devil. "Why?" he asked. "Why *me*?"

"Well, Mr. Hummell," the Devil responded. "You have qualities that I like and admire. You were unable to attain positions of power. Your life has taken several bad turns. However, your burning quest for power stayed intact, even when you became a beggar. Unfortunately, while your soul has endured and burned for revenge, your body has not. Your soul to say the least has always been older than your years. An ancient, cold soul. A very old and vengeful one. You will succumb to your injuries from the beating within a week. That is, unless you do this soul transformation. This will give you a new lease on life."

"But you are the Devil. You are evil."

"Mr. Hummell, there is no reason to get personal," the Devil replied. "Besides, you have not exactly been a saint yourself. Let's see, there was that boy in your first year of school you pushed down the stairs who died. Your mother was a prostitute who died from complications of syphilis. Your father was an abusive drunk and whore chaser who died from alcohol poisoning. You have committed numerous thefts and larcenies. Then there was the schoolgirl you raped while out for an evening during, on what is supposed to be the holiest night of the year. Although, she did have a questionable reputation. Or, how about the prostitute you strangled and then had sex with, in the back alley." The Devil laughed. "That poor bastard you blamed for it. I believe it was a beggar named Joseph Stromsky, who was like you are now. Beating him senseless near the scene was a very nice touch. I like that. The poor man still did not understand why he was being hung when they executed him. Or, how about the beggar who took you in and helped you out when you first hit the streets. What did you do? You paid him back by hitting him in the head with a rock and pushing him in the river. Those are some of the things that you did."

"You know about those?"

"Are the flames of Hell hot?" the Devil responded, with a grin. "Know of them. I was there at each and every one of them. I was a witness. I was in the shadows. Believe me, I was quite entertained. You have had a very colorful life of crime. You have been a thief of major and minor offenses, committed acts of child abuse, rape, assault and battery, embezzlement and murder."

"None of which was ever proved!" the beggar exclaimed defiantly.

"Aaahh, Mr.Hummell, spoken with all of the bravado and brashness of a barrister," replied the Devil. "I admire that quality about you."

"I did not think I was that bad, I had reasons for all of my actions."

"Of course, you did," the Devil commented, almost eerily reassuring. "The best part of all these incidents was that you managed to pull off all of these acts without a second thought or any guilt whatsoever. That takes a special talent, Mr. Hummell. That is what I need."

"I am what you need?" the beggar asked.

"Yes," the Devil replied. "You see, I too have limitations. I really cannot do anything without a willing participant's assistance to do my bidding. So, you see, Mr. Hummell, I too, am limited."

"So, you need me as well, huh?"

There was a long pause of silence and mutual understanding.

"I have never been needed," the beggar continued. "Not by anybody. Not in my whole life. It is not a feeling I have ever experienced before. I like it. A lot. It's empowering. So, what is in this for me?"

"Everything you ever dreamed of and more," the Devil responded.

The beggar grinned. "I'll do it." he agreed. "What happens to the little boy?"

"Do you really care, Mr. Hummell?" the Devil asked.

"No, not really," the Beggar answered. "I was just curious. Do you get his soul?"

"No, Unfortunately I do not," answered the Devil. Unless the child is an extreme exception, I lose out. But I make up for it elsewhere."

"So, what are the terms? My soul?"

"Eventually, if you choose," the Devil answered. "You see, I cannot just 'take' a soul.

They have to come to me willingly. For now, however, we are both getting what we want. I think you had better hide behind that building over there to surprise the boy."

"What is the incantation?" the beggar asked.

"Unum spiritus ergo nova corpus, abeo antiquus corpus unum spiritus," the Devil calmly and slowly answered.

"Which means?" the beggar asked.

"One soul, therefore new body, change to old body one spirit," the Devil answered.

"Unum, spiritus, ergo nova corpus," the beggar started to say from memory.

"Abeo antiquus ergo unum spiritus," the Devil concluded.

"Unum, spiritus ergo nova corpus abeo antiquus

corpus unum spiritus," the beggar smiled with great delight. Somehow, he found it easy to remember. "Now I just grab the boy and recite this three times."

The Devil just nodded and hissed, "Yesss."

The beggar nodded and decided to hide near a small shed-like building to wait for the boy. As dusk approached, a dark-haired little boy with clear blue eyes left the house. He stood outside of the house momentarily and bounced merrily on his way towards the building that the beggar was now hiding behind.

When the boy reached the building, the beggar jumped out from behind the building and grabbed the boy by the shoulders, startling him so much that he could not move.

"Unum spiritus ergo nova corpus abeo antiquus corpus unum spiritus," the beggar chanted as he held the boy tightly in his grip. As he continued the incantation, the sky seemed to turn red and the clouds rolled menacingly across it.

By the third repetition of the incantation, both the beggar and the boy felt like they had been struck by some kind of lightning. Both of their bodies shook and convulsed as they stood there together. The beggar felt like he was outside of his body and could see himself and the boy holding each other. He could also see pale transparent spirits floating around in the air all around them. The boy had lost consciousness. Soon, the beggar could feel the shock wearing off and he felt a little weak. But he also felt different. He did not hurt anymore. He felt rejuvenated. The little boy started to regain his senses. He hurt badly and was in pain. Tears started to flow out of his eyes from fear, confusion and pain.

The boy and the beggar stood there holding each other, not really knowing what happened. The two of them now stood looking at the bodies that had, moments earlier, been theirs.

Soon a woman in her early thirties, who was the boy's mother, came outside and yelled. "Get away from my son, you filthy beggar!"

The boy now broke away from the beggar's grip. The beggar now stood there confused and frightened.

"Adolph! Get away from that filthy beggar!" the mother yelled, and then picked up and threw a rock, hitting the beggar in the shoulder. She picked up another rock and threw it.

"Momma," the beggar cried softly as the tears of pain and fright flowed from a little boy who was now trapped in a dirty old beggar's body. He turned and ran away as best he could, sobbing as he did so. When he was well out of sight of the others, he collapsed from intense pain that engulfed his chest, and died.

The woman regained her composure and dusted herself off. "Now, Adolph you hurry up and get back in here!"

"So, Mr. Hummell, are you happy with your new body?" the Devil asked, already knowing the answer.

"It's better than I could have imagined," he answered happily. "So now what happens?"

"You live your new life," the Devil replied.

Just as the boy was about to say something, he looked up to see the spirit of the little boy he had replaced float upward towards the heavens.

"I see, Alfred Hummell is now officially dead," the boy said, with experience beyond his years.

"Most definitely," the Devil said. "The authorities will find him tomorrow. I am afraid that the shock of everything took its toll on the poor lad."

The boy turned to go back in the house and then stopped and paused. "Will I be seeing you again, in my life?" he asked.

"But, of course, Adolph," the Devil answered with a huge smile. "I am your generous benefactor and I would not dream of missing it."

Escape Artist

Ian Lane was an artist extraordinaire. His works with acrylics and oils was almost unparalleled in the current art scene. Not only was he great at painting, but he was quite adept at pen and ink, pencil, chalk and even watercolor.

His artwork was well-known, highly praised and sought out by art collectors, as well as the rich and famous. His talent as an artist was what enabled him to build a fortune and become a celebrity himself. Many thought he was quite the artist and personality, where women swooned over his ruggedly handsome looks.

He enjoyed the fame, notoriety and especially the adulation from just begin great at what he did. Ian knew he was great and played the part of the celebrity artist to the hilt.

But he was also now a convicted murderer. His fiery artistic temperament had led him to brutally murder his long-time girlfriend, Kimberly Jessup in one of his fits of rage during a heated argument where she threatened to leave him.

While his lawyer tried to argue that it was in the heat of passion and that he was diagnosed with a kind of bi-polar disorder, neither the judge nor the jury bought it. They viewed it as a desperate ploy by an attorney with no other defense for the accused. The prosecuting attorney pushed for the death penalty, but due his fame and notoriety, was given a fifty-years to life sentence.

At first Lane viewed this sentence as pretty much a death sentence, but eventually had to admit, while not great was still better than lethal injection or death in the electric chair by "Old Sparky."

Either way the sentence was still tough to take and not happy.

How could he be?

Fifty years in prison was going to be an eternity of despair, hopelessness, pain and anguish with no recourse for anything better or any change whatsoever. On top of that, he was going to be housed with the dregs and very worst of society. His only hope was as a celebrity prisoner that he would be kept away from the majority of prisoners or at least the psychotic and very dangerous ones.

He had no idea what lie in store for him as he was led to the warden's office by three large, burly prison guards. Lane was still stunned and in some shock by the verdict of his trial.

Once inside the warden's office he was greeted by a couple of serious and stern looking men in suits that he assumed was the warden and possibly an assistant as well as the chief of the prison guards.

The three prison guards dutifully one each side and behind him almost at full attention.

The assistant and the chief of the guards kept standing, while the warden quietly sat down in his chair behind his desk.

Ian was about to sit down in the chair in front of his desk but could tell by the warden's harsh glare that he was not allowed and that this chair was only reserved for non-inmates. He could not help but notice the assistant and the chief of the guards also giving the same disapproving look.

Ian thought better of his actions and remained standing. While he did not like this silent form of humiliations and intimidation, he decided it was the better part of valor to take it in this instance.

The warden looked down at the file on Ian on his desk, quietly nodding and pursing his lips as he did so. He quickly scanned over it, occasionally looking up at Ian with an expressionless face.

"Ian Lane," the warden finally stated. "You seem to be a high-profile prisoner in our facility."

"Yeah," Ian started to say, but stopped after seeing the warden's unyieldingly fierce glare.

"You will speak when spoken to and only when asked a direct question," the warden continued. "Is that clear?"

Hesitant to say anything, Ian silently nodded.

"For the record, I am Warden Phillip Washburn," the warden stated, introducing himself. He then pointed to the other two men. "That is my second in command, Deputy Warden Thomas Grimes and Chief of the Guards, Ronald Pine."

Ian nodded in acknowledgment.

"You are a ward of this facility," Warden Washburn continued. "This will be your home for at least fifty years as determined by your sentence. You will be subject to the rules and regulations of this facility just like the other prisoners. Do you understand?"

"Yes," Ian replied softly and hoarsely.

"Good," Washburn replied. "Due to your celebrity status we are forced to place you in a kind of partial quarantine with other high-profile and celebrity prisoners here."

Ian just nodded in agreement. While not thrilled or even happy to be here, he really did not want to mingle too much with the other hardened criminals.

"You will be put in that wing with the likes of other celebrity and high-profile prisoners," Washburn continued. "Some of your neighbors include mob boss Anthony DeNubba, hitman Joey Minella, killer, former leftwing activist Theodore Ryker, former actor Phillip Messner, plus a few others I am sure that you know of. Do you have any comments or questions?"

"Yes, Warden, I do," Ian replied. "First off, I will not be a problem. I shall follow the rules and be a model prisoner. I was just wondering if I could ask one courtesy."

"What is that?" Washburn asked.

"Could I be allowed to paint in my cell?" Ian asked. "I realize that I do not deserve or warrant it, but it's part of me. I will die if I cannot. It is all that I ask. I will not be a problem and give my word. I realize my word does not mean much considering I am a prisoner here, but I ask with all due respect and courtesy."

Washburn nodded then looked over at his deputy and chief of guards, both nodded in quiet agreement.

"I think we can accommodate that," Washburn responded. "However, you will be subject to random searches for contraband and weapons. Any infraction will result in the suspension of this privilege as long as we see fit. Do you understand?"

"Yes, sir," Ian said.

"This includes any violence, drug use, and any other rule infractions," Washburn added.

Ian nodded in agreement. He knew that being a model prisoner was necessary to get anything he needed. Ian hoped that it would not be as difficult as it sounded or could be.

"Good, now that we have that understanding and you have already been processed as a new prisoner, the guards will now take you to your new home," Washburn continued. "The only good news that I can give you is that you will be in a solitary cell. So, you will not be sharing a cell with anyone."

"Yes, Sir," Ian muttered.

"Very well," Washburn stated. "Gentlemen, please take our newest resident to his new home."

The guards quietly nodded in acknowledgment, then

led the new prisoner, Ian Lane to his cell.

As the guards led Ian through the prison, he did his best to keep looking straight ahead and not make any eye contact with any of the prisoners that were whistling, catcalling or making any other threatening or suggestive remarks at him. Try as he might to ignore it all, it was difficult, and he could not help but hear some of the remarks.

By the time Ian reached his cell, it had felt like it had been hours since he had left the warden's office, when it had actually only been twenty minutes at best.

Once in his cell, Ian sat down, closed his eyes and thought, "*I am in Hell. Maybe the death penalty would have been better than life in here.*"

Ian then stretched out on his bed, closed his eyes and drifted off to sleep. He was mentally, emotionally and physically spent. Ian knew that his daily routine in life would be dramatically different than it had been before.

He knew that he not only had to find a way to survive but also a way to exist and live.

But, for now he would get some much-needed sleep to try and recharge his personal batteries. That was first and foremost of what he needed right now.

Deep down Ian knew that he was fortunate. At least his cell block neighbors were people of some notoriety and fame. While bad, and killers in their own right, they were not nearly as disgusting as the general prison population. They were bad alright, but somehow, he found them more acceptable personally.

Still he knew that spending life in prison wasn't a great existence either. In fact, it flat out stunk. It was depressing. He felt like it was taking a little piece of his life each day. But at least it wasn't the death penalty. Ian knew that he had to do everything that he could to get out of here, either legally with his lawyer making continuous appeals or by some other means.

It didn't matter to him as long as he was out of here.

All Ian knew was that there was no way he was spending the rest of his life in this hell hole.

As for now he was just biding his time.

Ian just had to be patient and wait for the right opportunity.

For now, all Ian could do was ready himself mentally for the daily rigors and routine of a prison schedule. Never having had a strict schedule to follow before was going to be a whole different and eye-opening experience for him. He knew that it would be best to say and do as little as possible around the other inmates. There was no point in doing anything that could make him a target to any of the prisoners while he was there.

The first week of prison was an eye-opening experience for him. Ian learned quickly through observation and common sense of what to do and not do. He pretty much kept to himself, did not say a lot, took quick showers, answered politely and did his best to avoid any conflict and eye contact with other prisoners.

The worst part of being in prison was having to wake up at six a.m. for breakfast at 6:30. For most of his life he had not risen so early and at times was just going to bed then.

There was no way that he was going to get out of line and lose his painting privileges. They were too important to him.

By the second week, Ian visited the communal television room to watch a little television. Immediately upon entering the prisoners already in there took notice of the "newbie" entering the room.

Ian immediately noticed a big man sitting front and center was convicted mob boss Anthony "Tony" DeNubba. He was surrounded by two or three other bigger men. He noticed that DeNubba smiled at him. Ian looked for a place to sit, finally finding one he grabbed a chair at a table and did. He forgot how big and intimidating DeNubba was.

Ian looked around the room to see who else was in the room with him. He then looked to see what was on t.v. and noticed they were watching the World War Two movie, *The Great Escape.* He laughed to himself about the irony of that.

When the movie finally ended and there was a commercial break, Ian was approached by a slender, effeminate looking man with light brown hair and a wistful smile.

"I understand you are an artist," the man offered.

"Yes, I am," Ian replied, hesitantly, not knowing what to expect.

"You're also the one that killed his girlfriend, aren't you?" the man asked.

Ian nodded affirmatively

"Well, I am a bit of an artist myself," the man continued. "My name is Aidan. Aidan Peale. I actually draw. Mostly with pencil and sketches. It's kind of a hobby of mine. I was just wondering if we could be friends. Close personal friends. In this place we can all use good, close personal friends. You know, to watch over each other, be there for them and not be so lonely in a place like this."

Ian knew immediately what Aidan Peale was insinuating and why he had approached. Finally, after a few moments Ian replied. "Sorry, I'm not really interested. Nothing personal, but I'm afraid I don't swing that way."

Aidan looked both hurt and indignant over Ian's answer. But before he could say anything, a large burly man, with a face that looked like a clenched fist with hair, came over towards them. "Hey cupcake, quit bothering people!" he exclaimed. "Any trouble out of you and I'll pop your head like a zit, kapeesh?"

Aidan Peale looked both angry and frightened at the bigger man's intimidating presence. He wanted to say something but backed off quickly and beating a hasty retreat.

"Sorry to interrupt your introduction to *Zorro the Gay Blade* there, but Mr. DeNubba would like to have a word with you," the big man announced. "By the way, my name is Joey Minella. I am Mr. D's assistant."

"Don't you mean bodyguard?" Ian asked.

"That too," the big man replied. "It's just assistant sounded a little classier."

Both men chuckled.

"How I can I refuse an invite like that from such a man as Mr. DeNubba? Ian asked, but as more of a statement.

"Right," the big man agreed, with a broad smile on his face as he led the way to Anthony DeNubba.

"Ian Lane!" Anthony DeNubba exclaimed as he stood up and greeted Ian. "It has been a while!"

"It sure has," Ian agreed. "So, what can I do for you?"

"Well, it's more like what we can do for each other," DeNubba replied. "You see my wife bought a couple of your paintings when we were at one of your shows…"

"I remember," Ian said, interrupting DeNubba.

"Well, Marie is a fan of yours," DeNubba continued. "I have to say they are unique to say the least. It took a little while for me to get used to them, but after a while they grow on you and you appreciate their unusual scenic beauty. I have the one you titled *Hell's Paradise* in my office. I have to say it is a nice conversation piece. It really helped to make any people that came to see me a little more wary to say the least. The other one called *The Jungle* went into our living room. It really helped set the room off as Marie likes to say."

"Oh, yeah, I remember it well," Ian replied. "I always thought that was one of my best."

"Have a seat," DeNubba said. "So, we can talk."

"Okay," Ian responded as he sat down. "Thanks. So, what do you want?"

DeNubba smiled. "Well, I'd like to make you an offer," he continued. "Not one that you can't refuse, but one I think you will find acceptable."

"Okay."

"Well, my offer is that as long as I am in this place or even one of my associates you can be under my protection," DeNubba explained. "All it will cost you is a couple of paintings a year."

Ian listened and nodded. "That sounds fair," he replied. "I think we have a workable deal. Okay, that sounds like a deal."

"That's good," DeNubba responded. "That way Mr. Sissifus who killed his last couple of lovers after being jilted doesn't decide to carve his name in a heart into your chest. It seems he's the jealous type that doesn't take no for answer."

Ian laughed. "Thanks, I appreciate that."

"I thought you might like that," DeNubba commented. "Besides, even the bull queers stay away from that one. He's a real psycho. He just got out of the hole a short time ago for stabbing someone that rebuffed his advances."

"What happens if he refuses to take no for answer?" Ian asked.

"Then I will employ a couple of our darker skinned brothers that hate fags to handle him," DeNubba responded. "All I have to do is take care of their mammas and families with a few bucks and they will go medieval on his ass. So, that will be no problem. We know how to deal with the Sugar Plum Fairy. Or with anyone else that might be bothering you."

"Thanks, I appreciate that," Ian said.

"I thought you would go for that," DeNubba commented. "Besides, my wife is a big fan of yours and I thought I should do that, so she isn't so ticked at me being in the can. She wasn't exactly thrilled when I got sentenced. So, hopefully this will help make it a little better."

"Well, as soon as I get some painting supplies, you tell Marie that I will have a painting for her in about a month, give or take a few days," Ian replied.

DeNubba smiled, reached over and patted Ian on the back. "Thanks," he said. "Welcome to the fold."

"So, what's on next?" Ian asked.

"*Goodfellas*," DeNubba replied.

"Oh, a classic," Ian laughed. "Sounds good."

Ian now felt a little more safe and secure since his arrival in prison. By the time the film ended, Ian felt a lot better about being under the protective umbrella of DeNubba and his associates. He still knew that he had to be careful but at least it felt like someone at least had his back.

It was somewhat ironic that he was safe in a clique of convicted mobsters.

Yet, even with that, Ian still knew that Aidan Peale was lurking around, upset and indignant that Ian had not accepted his overtures of a relationship.

Ian could tell that he was a man that did not take rejection very well and was possessive of what he considered his. That was the main thing that concerned him, at least up to this point about being in prison.

He hoped that by keeping a low profile, keeping to himself and not pissing anybody off kept him out of harm's way.

The next few weeks were routine and mundane for Ian. So, much, that all Ian could think if Hell was repetition, then this place was definitely it.

Hell.

Pure Hell.

Every day was strictly scheduled and monitored. The only place where security was not as prevalent was in the bathroom near the showers and even that was monitored to the point where if you were in there too long the guards checked on you.

It seemed like "the bulls" were always around and present, looking over your shoulder.

While it wasn't always true, it sure seemed like it.

There was still the occasional "shanking" or stabbing of fellow inmates.

Ian did his best to keep his nose down, not argue or offend any of the other prisoners while keeping his guard up. But with the protection offered him by Tony DeNubba and his associates he wasn't always as alert as he once had been.

He had almost forgotten about Aidan Peale.

That is until one day when they reached the showers at the very same time. Aidan just quietly smiled and nodded at him in what appeared to be a friendly, non-threatening manner acknowledging way. While still wary and cautious of him, Ian briefly turned his back on him while he washed his body. When he turned around, Ian noticed that Aidan was gone.

Ian felt a little better about being in there the same time as Aidan. A quiet sense of relief filled him, since he did not want to deal with Aidan and the drama about being rejected by him with regards to a prison relationship.

He just hoped Aidan got over it.

So far, he appeared to have.

He could only hope.

By the time Ian stepped out of the shower to put on his prison uniform, Aidan was nowhere in sight. He figured that Aidan had changed and left the dressing room area.

As Ian started to get dressed, he turned and faced the locker, where his clothes were hanging up.

When half-dressed, he appeared out of nowhere, pushing Ian into the lockers. Before Ian could react or defend himself, Aidan plunged a sharpened metal shiv into his left side. Ian cried out in pain just before collapsing on the floor, unconscious.

The next thing Ian knew was that he was in the prison infirmary, heavily sedated and drowsy from the emergency surgery that he had just underwent. At least for now the painkillers and sedatives had gotten the pain down to a dull, but constant throb. He also noticed one of the medical personnel standing over him.

"Wha..where am I?" he struggled to ask. "What happened?"

"Relax," the man said. "I'm Physician's Assistant Michael Laslovick. You're a very lucky man. One of the other prisoners stabbed you with a makeshift blade. A shiv is what I believe they call it. It punctured your lung. Fortunately, a guard was nearby and heard you cry out. He prevented you from being killed."

"Oh," Ian muttered, hoarsely and still only partially unconscious.

Even still sedated, and groggy Ian knew who the perpetrator was that stabbed him.

"Just relax and take it easy," Laslovick instructed.

"How long have I been here?" Ian asked.

"You've been here for over a day," Laslovick replied. "You will be confined to a bed for a while until you recover. Oh, by the way, just call me Dr. Mike. That's what everyone calls me."

"Okay," Ian groaned. "Thanks."

"Try and get some rest," Laslovick said. "Also try not to move much, you've got some stitches both internally and externally. Well, I'll be back shortly."

Ian quietly nodded affirmatively to the physician's assistant before slipping off to sleep again.

When Ian finally woke up again most of the anesthesia had worn off and he was feeling the sharp pain of the wound caused by Aidan Peale's blade handiwork. As Ian inhaled, he seethed in pain, grimacing and groaning.

"You need another shot?" Laslovick asked, upon seeing Ian grimace in pain.

Ian nodded. "Yeah," he muttered, still seething in pain.

"Okay," Laslovick announced. "Here comes your shot."

Ian nodded. "Thanks," he muttered.

Laslovick quietly nodded as he administered the shot to help ease Ian's pain. "The doctor will change the bandage tomorrow and take a look at how the wound is healing."

"Thanks," Ian muttered hoarsely, still seething in pain.

"It should kick in soon," Laslovick added.

"Good, I hope so," Ian said, still grimacing.

"You will be having some visitors later," Laslovick announced. "The warden and deputy warden will be in to see you later."

"Yeah," Laslovick added. "They want to see if you're alright. I think they also want to possibly find out if you plan on any retribution."

Ian coughed and winced from the pain. "Not hardly," he seethed. "I want to keep my painting privileges. It's the only thing that keeps me going in here and I don't want to lose that."

Laslovick quietly nodded affirmatively before leaving to check on his other convict patients.

After lunch Warden Washburn and Deputy Warden Grimes paid Ian a visit. Washburn and Grimes stood on each side of Ian's bed almost as if they were doctors on grand rounds talking with a patient.

"How are you doing?" Washburn asked.

"I'm alright," Ian replied. "It hurts, but I'm alright."

"I regret this happened to you," Washburn added. "We'll make every effort to see that it does not happen again."

"I appreciate that," Ian muttered. "I know that you cannot guarantee it, but I do appreciate it nonetheless."

"We hope that you are not planning some kind of retaliation," Washburn continued. "Otherwise you will have your painting privileges revoked."

Ian exhaled. At least the painkillers had finally kicked in and he could breathe better. "No," he finally groaned. "I have no intentions of seeking any kind of retribution against Aidan Peale."

"That's good," Washburn said, nodding.

"You see my painting privileges mean too much to me," Ian continued. "And I do not want to lose it. I'd might as well be dead then. I'd rather be in here than lose my painting privileges."

The warden and his deputy looked at each other.

"When you are released from here, which should be in a few weeks, I think we can establish your painting privileges then," Washburn announced.

"Thanks, Warden," Ian said. "That means a lot. I told you that I gave my word that there would be no trouble and I intend to keep it."

"Yes, you have," Washburn admitted. "I believe you have earned that privilege when you leave here."

With that Washburn and Grimes left Ian's bedside.

"Well, he sure values his painting," Grimes commented.

"It's all he has left," Washburn replied. "It's what keeps him alive."

"You've got a point," Grimes agreed.

"It's really the one thing he has left that he was able to do outside of here that he can do in here," Washburn continued. "I believe him when he says without it, he would die."

A couple of hours after the Warden and his deputy left, he was paid a visit by one of Tony DeNubba's associates.

"Hello, Mr. Lane," the man announced. "I'm Rocco Scalise, Mr. DeNubba wanted me to come and see how you are doing. He offers his best regards and sympathies about what happened to you."

"Oh."

"He wanted to add that he thought it best that he not, visit personally, and thought that you would understand," Rocco continued. "You know for obvious reasons. He also told me to tell you that the Sugar Plum Fairy will not do this to you again once he is released from Solitary confinement. In fact, he guarantees it. So, don't worry when he is released. He will be taken care of."

Ian could only imagine what that meant and did not want to know any of the details to that. He figured it was better to not know and play ignorant.

"Thank, Mr. DeNubba for me," Ian finally replied. "Also tell him that I greatly appreciate it and I will have a painting for him as soon as I can, once I start painting again."

"No problemo," Rocco said. "I had better be going before the screws wonder why I was here."

"Oh, yeah," Ian said, nodding in agreement.

The next few weeks were pretty non-eventful for Ian. He could not do much of anything except try to heal from his knife wound while being confined to the infirmary. All he could really do was read, sketch a little watch some television. Some days he felt like he was ready to go back to his cell, while other days his wound ached terribly.

At least now he could breathe without hurting but the area around the wound was still tender where any wrong movement would cause him to wince and grimace in pain. Every time he did so, Ian thought of what Rocco had told him what was in store for Aidan Peale. The more he thought about it, the more Ian did not care what happened to Aidan Peale. In fact, he hoped it was painful and that he suffered greatly.

Ian knew it was all a matter of time before he heard anything. Ian figured that Aidan Peale would be out of solitary confinement about some time after he was going to get out of the infirmary. When exactly he did not know but knew it could be anytime. So, he knew that Aidan Peale was a dead man walking upon his release from solitary confinement.

Ian just looked forward to the news of Aidan Peale's demise.

All he had to do was feign any knowledge of it so he privileges wouldn't be revoked.

By the time Ian had been cleared to leave the infirmary a few days over a month had passed since the stabbing incident. As soon as he returned to his cell, Ian began his first painting since arriving in prison. It was for Tony DeNubba's wife, just as he agreed to do.

Ian thought it would be best to paint her something warm and welcoming, possibly even cheerful for her. If it made her happy then he knew Tony DeNubba would be happy as well.

After a couple of weeks, Ian was a little less than

halfway done. He figured the general slowness of his progress was due to the fact he had been somewhat out of practice. This was really his first painting since he had killed his girlfriend. So, he had to allow for that. Soon enough though, his painting and muscle memory kicked in and he was able to regain his old form.

After another couple of weeks, Ian had progressed to the point of being mostly done with the painting.

Ian had also heard rumors that Aidan Peale was due to get out of solitary confinement soon. He was confident that something would soon happen to him soon after his release from solitary. Ian was almost certain of it.

In fact, Ian could hardly wait for it.

When Ian received the news of Aidan Peale's death he was nearly finished with his painting. The prisoner in the cell next to him told him.

"Well, you won't have to worry about that gay blade anymore," said the inmate, a convicted murderer and former actor known as Josh Haskins. "Some of the suntans got him in the shower and did a real number on him."

"Wow," Ian replied, acting like he did not know about it.

"You're not sorry, are you?" Haskins asked.

"Well, considering that the man stabbed me, hell no," Ian responded. "I just hope it was as painful as my stabbing was."

Haskins roared at Ian's answer. This caused Ian to laugh as well.

For the moment and all things considered, Ian felt pretty good about his life.

Later that week, Ian was summoned to the Warden's office. Once there he saw the deputy warden and the chief of the guards.

"Take a seat," Washburn ordered.

Ian sat down, almost knowing what the meeting was about. He decided it was best to not say or ask anything before the warden said anything.

"I assume you heard about Aidan Peale," Washburn continued.

"Yes, I did," Ian admitted. "I can't say I am sorry."

"We have reason to believe this was in retaliation for your stabbing," Washburn added.

"Really?" Ian asked.

"We know that you are close to Tony DeNubba and seem to be under his protection," Washburn stated.

"Warden, to be fair, I had met Mr. DeNubba outside of prison," Ian responded. "He and his wife bought a couple of my paintings. So, we have met before in passing. That was the extent of our relationship. I have nothing to hide there and will admit we are acquaintances."

Washburn nodded. "We know that one of his associates came to see you in the infirmary," he continued. "We believe it was in retaliation for Aidan Peale's stabbing you."

"Yes, I was visited by, Rocco Scalise," Ian admitted. "But it was to send his regards and that there was no hurry on me doing a painting for his wife. I had told him I would do one earlier for him when and if my painting privileges were given. That was it."

"So, you expect us to believe you had no part in the death of Aidan Peale?" Deputy Warden Grimes asked.

"I cannot help whether you do or not," Ian responded. "I have only been here a short time and still learning my way around. I try to keep my head down and stay out of trouble. I don't talk much and keep to myself to avoid problems. Yet, in spite of all that I still ended up being stabbed by someone who has stabbed others before I even arrived. So, please excuse me if I'm not sorry the little bastard is dead. As far as I'm concerned, he got whatever he deserved."

"That's pretty cold," Washburn snapped. You're not sorry he was brutally beaten to death."

"Would you be?" Ian retorted. "Would you be, had it been you that he stabbed, really? Sorry, but my response is going to be honest. I'm damn glad he's dead. That way I don't have to look over shoulder every time he was nearby. Did I do it or have a hand in it? No. Absolutely not. Just don't ask me to be sorry about it. As bad as jail is, I still value my life and want to live."

"I see your point," Washburn said. "I have to admit you have got me there. I would probably feel the same way as you, had it been me. But, if we ever find out that you were involved in any way or even knew about this, I will permanently revoke your painting privileges."

"I understand," Ian replied. "I would never do anything to jeopardize that. It means too much to me."

Washburn eyed Ian warily. Deep down he thought Ian knew more than he was telling, but also knew that Ian had been honest in his reaction to Aidan Peale's death. "Okay," he finally said. "You will keep your painting privileges for now, that is unless something new comes to light on this."

"I appreciate that fact," Ian replied.

"Just know we will be keeping a close eye on you, and if we find anything at all you, your painting days are finished," Washburn warned. "Okay, we're done here."

The guards then escorted Ian back to his cell.

Once he left the Warden's Office, Ian knew that he would be under a lot more scrutiny than he already was. He knew that Warden Washburn suspected him and DeNubba of doing something about Aidan Peale. Ian knew that he just had to go about his business as if nothing happened.

Right now, he was focused on doing the painting for

Tony DeNubba's wife. That was first and foremost on his mind.

In spite of the boring and mundane rigors of everyday prison life, Ian was somehow able to immerse himself in his painting. The more he worked on it, the more alive he felt. Painting gave him a sense of freedom that the four walls of the prison could not contain. His only interruptions had been meals, duties and some activities when he knew that a break was necessary. Plus, the increased searches of his cell delayed him but only for a short time.

His intense passion and desire for his work helped him to complete his artwork sooner than originally expected.

He wanted to wait another week before presenting it to DeNubba. This was his usual methodical practice when it came to painting. Finish, then set aside for a week to make sure there was nothing else to add, and if there was something, do it then. Even if the painting was for someone like DeNubba, he would be no exception to this rule.

This was also why his work was appreciated. He wanted his work to be flawless and nearly perfect before letting anyone else see it. Being in prison would not change his artistic routine.

Ian stood back observing his latest magnum opus. He decided to name it *Sunset Over Paradise* which featured orange, red, yellow sunset over an almost darkened and somewhat silhouetted tropical island paradise.

Ian took a deep breath. He was filled with a great sense of satisfaction at the completion of his artwork. He felt it was his best in quite some time.

He regretted having to give it away, but that was sometimes the price one had to pay at times in life. Especially, here in prison where it could be the difference between life and death. Ian had already come as close to death as he wanted to in here. Giving away a painting to ensure his safety and survival was a small price to pay.

It was a sacrifice he was all too willing to make.

He would take the painting to DeNubba when he thought it was completely finished. He hoped that his wife would be visiting soon. From what he knew, she visited her husband twice a month, so it had to be soon.

Another week of prison life and routine went by as Ian put the finishing touches on his painting. It was finally done. He could breathe a sigh of relief. When Ian finally decided to show it to DeNubba, he was quite impressed.

"Wow!" DeNubba exclaimed. "I'm no art connoisseur but that is damn fine work. From what I have seen, it is amongst your best."

"Thank you."

"No, seriously," DeNubba continued. "It's spectacular."

Rocco and Joey looked at the painting and were impressed as well.

"It's a beaut," Rocco commented.

"Very nice," Joey added.

"Marie will love it," DeNubba said. "She'll be here Saturday."

"I'm glad you like it," Ian commented. "Thanks for everything."

"Forget about it," DeNubba exclaimed, almost sounding like a stereotypical mobster from the films. "It's great. She'll be pleased. Very pleased. I'm telling you guys they don't get any better than this."

Both Joey and Rocco nodded in agreement.

"You know the warden was leaving no stone unturned to find out who killed Aidan Peale," DeNubba explained. "He had me and the boys in for interrogation. He suspects we had a hand in it. But he'll never find out.

You see the niggers don't like the queers for the most part either, especially Peale."

"I kind of figured," Ian replied.

"Plus, a lot of people suspected Peale was a rat," DeNubba added. "That fact pissed off a lot of people too."

"I don't doubt that either," Ian admitted.

"Well, that's the way the twinky crumbles, I guess," DeNubba roared.

Ian laughed at DeNubba's remark about Peale.

"Hey boss, the movie is about to start in the TV room," Rocco announced.

"You joining us?" DeNubba asked.

"Sure, what's on?" Ian asked.

"*Some Like It Hot*," DeNubba replied. "I always liked that one even if it made fun of the business a little."

"Me too," Ian admitted.

After watching the movie, the next few weeks were pretty routine for Ian. It was all hellish repetition. The only thing different was the fact that he was starting preliminary work for his next painting. He also found out from DeNubba that his wife really loved the painting. Ian was glad about that fact. At least he had some powerful friends in prison and that was good.

During this quiet time, Ian was visited by his attorney Harris Michelson. Because of attorney-client privilege they were able to meet alone, without fear of being recorded or overheard.

"How are you doing, Ian?" Michelson asked. "You look good considering."

"Yeah, I'm good," Ian admitted.

"I was here immediately after you were knifed," Michelson explained. "You were pretty groggy and out of it when I was. I did manage to get the warden to keep you I the infirmary until you were completely recovered."

"You were?" Ian asked. "They might have told me, but I was out of it. Thanks for visiting me just the same."

"Hey that's what I'm here for," Michelson said. "Is there anything I can do for you or something that you need?"

"Yeah, there is," Ian snapped. "You can get me out of here. This place is Hell."

"Yeah, sorry about that," Michelson said, nodding. "I've filed some appeals. We can only wait and see. I think they're strong cases for appeal though. I'll do my best to extradite the process. I know it hasn't been easy."

"That's an understatement," Ian groaned. "You can't even begin to imagine how bad it is."

"I realize that," Michelson countered. "I'm doing everything I can. Unfortunately, the wheels of justice grind slowly."

"That's for damn sure," Ian muttered. "Any slower and a snail would be passing us."

"I'll see what I can do," Michelson added. "I'll try to call in some favors to expedite the process. Well, I have to go. I have some more appeals to file on your behalf."

"Good," Ian said. "Do whatever you can. This place is a hell hole."

"I'll do everything I can," Michelson said. "Try and stay strong."

"Is there any other way to be?" Ian asked in response.

Michelson nodded and then left, as Ian was escorted back to his cell.

While not overly satisfied with their monthly meeting, Ian knew Michelson was right. His case was no different. Ian knew the appeal process would take some time.

About a week after their meeting, Ian received a letter from Marie DeNubba, thanking him for the exquisite artwork. He greatly appreciated the thoughtful and considerate letter. Ian was so touched by the letter that he decided to keep it.

Some weeks later, Ian received a visit from his agent Morgan Latimer. Latimer was a tall, lanky man with a kind of baby face hidden behind a start of a beard that looked unkept and unshaven more than anything else.

"It's been a while," Latimer said to Ian through the visitor glass. "How are you doing?"

"So, what brings this visit?" Ian asked. "I haven't seen you since before the trial. What's up?"

"For one thing, I wanted to see how you were doing," Latimer replied. "Are you alright?"

"Yeah," Ian responded. "As well as could be expected. So, what brings this visit after all of this time."

Latimer shifted in the chair, noticeably uncomfortable. "Well…" he started to say.

"Spit it out," Ian snapped. "Let's hear it."

"Well, it's like this, Ian," Latimer started again. "I have to drop you as a client. I have done all that I can do for you and with this murder conviction there is nothing that I can do for you. I'm truly sorry, but that's the way it has to be."

Ian sat seething and glaring at Latimer. He wanted to kill him. "So, now you're dropping me after all of the money that I have made you," he snapped. "So, much for loyalty I guess, huh?"

"It's not like it's unwarranted," Latimer countered. "I'm not dropping you for no reason at all. Right now, you're about as marketable as O.J. Simpson. Nobody is interested in a convicted murderer's artwork. So, tell me how I'm supposed to market that."

Ian took a deep breath and exhaled. "Great!" he spat. "Just great. Thanks for nothing, Morgan."

"Look, I should have done this a long time ago," Latimer admitted. "You and that so-called artistic temperament of yours. It only works well when dealing with painting, not people. Your so-called artistic temperament was just an excuse to be an abusive, cruel and violent jerk. So, blame yourself. I should have done something way sooner. Way, way sooner. Before you became the monster, you are now."

"Cry me a river," Ian muttered, his voice dripping with sarcasm.

"I should have put a stop to you sooner," Latimer continued, shaking his head. "Now I too have blood on my hands. I have the blood of Kimberly on my hands too, thanks to my own inaction. I should have stopped you a long time ago. I knew you were bad, but sat back and let the money roll in. I don't know who's more pathetic me or you. I just wish I had been able to walk away clean from you. May God forgive me, but I am guilty of enabling you."

Ian just stared blankly at Latimer who was now glaring back at his former client. Finally, after a few seconds Latimer got up and left. He had done what he came here to do.

Ian sat a few more moments seething with anger, stewing in his hatred.

If Ian could have killed him then and there he would have. But for now, all Ian could do was wish Morgan Latimer dead.

Latimer's dropping him as a client deeply bothered Ian. He had been the first to truly believe in him as well as giving him a chance. Latimer was the one that helped put Ian's name on the map and later fortune and fame.

Ian was now hurt, angry, and definitely uncertain about his artistic future. Morgan Latimer had finally seen to that.

This put Ian in a very dark place mentally. A state that he would remain in for a quite some time. It was even reflected in his latest painting that he titled *Hell.* By the time he had finished three months had passed by.

During this time, he noticed that Tony DeNubba didn't seem as energetic and exuberant as he once had. He seemed a bit tired and down. Ian figured that maybe he received some bad news like he had with his agent. Either way, Ian wasn't going to press the issue with him.

A few days later when Ian showed up to the t.v. room only to see Joey and Rocco quietly and sullenly sitting in front of the television but not really watching it, he knew something was wrong.

"What's wrong, guys?" Ian asked. "Where's Tony?"

Both men looked at Ian with deep sadness. After a few moments Joey responded. "Mr. DeNubba died. He went to sleep last night and didn't wake up. Massive heart attack."

"Wow!" Ian gasped, shocked by the announcement. "I am truly sorry."

Both men nodded in acknowledgment sadly.

A kind of quiet unspoken horror and dread began to fill Ian. His sense of safety and security that he had as a friend of Tony DeNubba's began to rapidly diminish. He felt sick in the pit of his stomach. It also sank into him that Tony DeNubba was also one of the few friends that he ever had.

Now he was gone.

His whole prison life and situation changed in just one day.

Once In returned to his cell, he sat down and wrote Marie DeNubba a very thoughtful condolence letter. He then proceeded to paint her a very flattering portrait of her husband using a picture of him and his memory. He somehow managed to finish the portrait in a week. He then sent it to her with his condolences.

After that Ian kept his head down and stayed to himself.

If prison was hell before, then somehow, he had fallen even deeper into the pits of it.

A couple of months later while staring blankly at a canvas, fighting for some kind of inspiration, a special package arrived for him. It had naturally been searched to make sure there was no contraband, drugs or weapons.

"It's paints, Rembrandt," the prison guard that delivered the package said. "Oh, and you also have a visitor.

"A visitor?" Ian asked, who took the box and rummaging through it. He found several containers of paints with no brand names of any kind on them. They were only marked with the colors that they were.

"Yeah, a visitor," the guard replied. "You had better go see them."

Ian decided that he had better go see who this mysterious visitor was. When he arrived in the visitors' area, he was greeted by the sight of somewhat familiar face that he recognized as Marie DeNubba.

More than a little surprised he sat down across from here. "Mrs. DeNubba," he said hesitantly. "I am so very sorry for your loss."

"Please call me Marie," she replied. "Did you get the paints? Did you like them?"

"Yes," Ian responded. "Thank you. I just received them. Of course, they had to search them. But you did not have to do that."

"Of course," she responded, matter-of-factly. "And you did not have to do a portrait of my Tony either and yet you did."

"So, Marie, what brings this visit?" Ian asked.

"I wanted to tell you about these paints," Marie Denubba replied. "The place I bought them from is a specialty store. It is called *Oddities and Ends*. The proprietor said these paints have special properties. Special magical properties. I thought these might come in handy while you're here."

"Really?" Ian asked.

"Yes," Marie continued. "They said that the artist could paint scenery of places where they would like to be and somehow be there. It's those special magical properties they told me about."

"Thank you," Ian replied, somewhat stunned. "I am deeply humbled and thankful for the gift."

"You were one of Tony's few friends," Marie responded. "You may not have realized it, but he really liked you. He thought of you as a friend. A good friend. One of the few that he really had. He always enjoyed watching the movies and talking to you. Especially the non-business-related stuff. I feel that he died with a good friend nearby. One that wasn't in the business. He thought a man of your talents should not be in here."

"Yeah," Ian agreed. "We had some good times watching the movies."

"Anyway, paint where you would like to escape to," Marie continued. "Paint a place where you would like to be and hide out at. Paint some kind of freedom for yourself. I have to go now but take care Ian. God bless you."

Ian watched as Marie DeNubba stood up, then walked away. Now he was truly intrigued by the paints that she had sent him. On top of that she was imploring him to paint some that he could escape to. He wasn't certain whether she was just mad with grief over her husband's passing or legitimately trying to help him get out of prison. Part of his mind thought of the old Bugs Bunny cartoons where someone painted a door and entered it. He thought she was talking about something a little more detailed than that cartoon.

Either way he was about to find out how these paints

could help him like she suggested.

As soon as Ian returned to his cell, he began to think about all of the places that he visited and which one he enjoyed the most. Which one did he actually consider his personal escape? He asked himself over and over again.

After a few minutes it came to him.

The place that he always loved and enjoyed the most had been his grandfather's cabin that was nestled in the woods near a small lake. It was peaceful and quiet. To him, it was perfect.

If he had to have a place to escape to, that would be it. He smiled as he thought of the times he, his dad, and his grandfather went there and took the old rowboat out into the lake to fish.

To Ian they were fond memories.

He decided to use the four by six-foot canvas that he had made earlier for this particular painting. Ian started immediately to paint the place of his dreams. He only needed his minds' eye to capture it on canvas.

For the next few weeks using every spare moment that he had, Ian worked on his painting. It was as much a labor of love as it was an escape from the harsh realities of prison.

By the time he had finished with every minute and intricate detail of the place, Ian was both ecstatic and a bit sad.

As Ian stepped back to study his latest work, he wondered what Marie DeNubba had been talking about. There was nothing magical or different about the paints that he could see. Ian was disappointed at least for the moment. He thought it was just the ramblings of an overwrought and grieving widow.

"What else could you expect?" he asked himself.

Later that night, after lights out and Ian was lying on his cot sleeping, he felt soft summer breeze blowing on him, He also felt sunlight shining on him. It was warm and welcoming to him.

Even peaceful.

It felt good.

Ian turned looking over at his painting. Still groggy and his eyes half-opened, he thought it looked like the sunlight and the breeze were emanating from the painting he had just completed. This snapped Ian out of his half-asleep state. He quickly sat up, asking "What the Hell?" before finally moving towards the painting.

The painting itself looked so very much alive and real. The trees were moving in the breeze and the water had ripples on it. He felt the warm breeze and the sunlight on his skin.

At first, Ian thought he was still dreaming.

Ian then reached out to touch the painting only to have his right hand and wrist actually go into it. He then pulled it out and did the same thing with his left hand.

"Incredible," he gasped, in astonishment.

Ian knew then that this was the special magical properties that Marie DeNubba was talking about. This was she was so adamant about him painting something with these paints.

Ian then removed the painting from its easel, placing it on the floor against his bed so that it sat upright. He stood looking at the portrait. It seemed to beckon to him. He felt a strong longing to go there.

Now was his chance for escape. It was nighttime and the guards had already done their headcount. Ian thought for a moment. Before he escaped, he had better grab some personal effects, like the paints, some brushes and other items and carry them through with him during his escape. As he bundled them up in an old shirt, Ian got on his knees. He then crawled towards the painting.

Once inside the painting, Ian was in the world that he

had painted. It was beautiful. The air was pure, the waters clear and the woods pristine. Nestled inside the tree line near some large spruces, white pines, mighty oaks and a few birches was the cabin. It was all so beautiful and fresh.

It looked fresh and new. Everything was better than he remembered.

"Wow," Ian gasped as he looked around at his new-found paradise.

Best of all he felt free.

That was something he hadn't felt in quite some time.

Ian raised his hands in the air in celebration "Yes!" he exclaimed. "The artist has escaped. I'm an escaped artist. Better yet, I am an escape artist."

Ian laughed out loud at his own pun.

He then decided to explore his newly created world and new home. He could hardly contain his euphoria of being free.

The next morning when the guards made their rounds and found Ian Lane not in his cell, they alerted the warden and conducted a massive prison search. As the authorities searched the grounds and the prison, the warden paid Ian's cell a visit.

Nobody could figure out how Ian had escaped. They could find no traces of him anywhere. Even outside of the prison and statewide search.

It's like he just disappeared," Deputy Warden Grimes commented in Ian's cell.

"Nobody just disappears, Tom," Warden Washburn snapped. "He wasn't Houdini. He has to be somewhere."

"I'd like to know how he did it," the Chief-of-the Guards Pine commented.

"Me too," Grimes agreed.

"I'd rather see him caught," Warden Washburn muttered.

Grimes picked up the last painting that Ian had done.

"He was definitely a great artist," he observed.

Washburn looked at the painting. "That he was, Tom, that he was," he agreed. "But he's an *escaped* artist, not an *escape* artist. He will turn up somewhere."

Grimes' cellphone rang. He answered it. "Yes," He then listened. "Really? Well that might be difficult. Since he seems to have escaped. Tell his lawyer that we are currently conducting a search for him."

"Who was that?" Washburn asked.

"It seems Mr. Lane's lawyer was able to get a retrial on a technicality and the court ordered his temporary release," Grimes announced.

"How ironic," Washburn commented. "Ron, have this painting burned. I do not want Ian Lane to ever make money on his artistic endeavors while he was in prison."

"Yes, Sir," Pine replied. "I see to it personally."

"Thank you," Washburn said.

Pine along with his two top captains, David Fletcher and Jim Runnels took the painting to the incinerator and placed it inside. They stood back and watched as the flames engulfed the painting.

Meanwhile inside the painting Ian Lane screamed in abject agony and horror as his world came burning down around him while he was in it. He knew immediately what was happening and there was no escape for him.

"Did you hear that?" Pine asked, upon hearing muffled screams

"Yeah," Runnels replied. "What is that?"

"It's probably one of the inmates getting theirs' in the next cell block," Fletcher suggested.

"Great more paperwork," Runnels muttered.

"That's probably all it is," Pine agreed as they watched the painting burn and Ian Lane's world and last masterpiece turn to ashes.

From Forever to Eternity

The storm raged with an uncontrolled, violent fury. The dark clouds had turned mid-afternoon as dark as night. Thunder echoed throughout the heavens as web-shaped lightning flashed across the rain-filled sky, as the wind helped to reign havoc across the great lake.

The little ship was at the mercy of nature's most dangerous elements and in great peril as waves pounded angrily against it. Battered and beaten by the rain, wind and wave, the ship stood little chance against the horrific storm.

Drenched by wind, pounded by waves, and battered by relentless winds the ship and its crew were little more than prey for the storm from Hell and began to sink beneath the depth of dark, cold waters. The crews' death screams muted by the raging storm.

Paul Landon sat up in his bunk screaming out in terror and pain. He looked around realizing that he was in his cabin aboard his ship. As he wiped away the sweat from his brow, he realized that he had another nightmare and any thought of trying to get any sleep an exercise in futility.

"Dear, God not again," he moaned, still shaking from the horrible dream. "Not again, please, not again."

There was a knock on his cabin door, and it opened. "Are you alright, Sir," asked crewman Chester Blakeslee.

"Yeah, I'm alright," Paul groaned in return.

"Another bad dream?" Chester asked.

"Yeah," Paul replied. "The same damn one."

"I just happened to be passing by again, when I heard you call out," Chester explained. "It's almost time for your watch."

"Alright," Paul grumbled as he got out of bed. "I'll be there as soon as I'm dressed."

"Yes, Sir, I'll tell the captain," Chester said before closing the cabin door.

Once on deck Paul looked pale and exhausted. Simply put, he was dead tired with every bit of it showing up on his face and body.

Captain Jacob Vanderdecker, a bellicose and somewhat belligerent man was both taken aback and irritated by his second-in-command's appearance.

"Mr. Landon, I hope your appearance doesn't continue to be a habit," Captain Vanderdecker sternly warned. "Because I may be forced to find a replacement."

Paul lowered his head and humbly said, "Yes, Sir, I shall do my best to see it doesn't happen anymore."

"Make sure that it does," Vanderdecker warned.

"It's just a matter of not sleeping very well," Paul explained.

"Yes, so I've heard," Vanderdecker replied. "This makes how many nights you've woke up screaming? Is there something wrong, Mr. Landon? Because I cannot have my second-in-command suffering from nightmares every night."

Paul took a deep breath and then exhaled. "I don't know, Captain," he finally said.

"What do you mean you don't know?" Vanderdecker asked. "Just what exactly are your nightmares about?"

Paul hesitated for a moment. "They involve us being lost in a terrible storm," he finally explained. "Just like the one we just experienced."

"Well, Mr. Landon, we came through that one just fine," Vanderdecker said. "Look around you. Do we look like we have sunk during a storm? We have had nothing but calm weather. We have had clam waters and fair winds. Each day has been identical to the next after that storm, so you have nothing to worry about."

"If you say so, Sir," Paul said.

"You doubt me, Mr. Landon?" Vanderdecker asked.

"No, Sir," Paul replied. "It's just that we've been sailing these waters ever since the storm and haven't gotten anywhere. Doesn't it seem strange to you that we haven't arrived at our destination yet, Captain? We haven't seen land or ship since before the storm."

"So, what are you saying, Mr. Landon?" Vanderdecker asked. "Because we are right here in flesh and blood on a ship. Now I suggest you go below and get some food and plenty of coffee in you. You're no good to me the way you are."

"Yes, Sir," Paul said, glumly.

As Paul sat in the galley filling up on strong black coffee and eating a couple of biscuits with salt pork he could not help but notice how cold and weather-beaten it appeared below deck. He touched the inside part of the hull and it felt cold and wet. Dank and chilled like a tomb he thought

"So how are you doing?" asked a familiar voice.

Paul looked up and saw it was his friend and second mate Phillip Laird. He sat down across from Paul shaking his head. "Tsk, tsk, tsk, what are we going to do with you?" he asked.

"Shut up and leave me alone," Paul replied.

"Now is that for any way for you to act when your best friend is concerned?" Phillip asked. "I was just checking on you to see how you were doing."

"I'm okay, I guess," Paul muttered. "Did the captain

want you to check on me?"

"No," Phillip answered. "You haven't been the same since the storm. You've had nightmares every night since. So, I'd say I'm a little concerned. You're looking like hell from the lack of sleep."

"So, what do you want me to say?" Paul asked, before taking a sip of coffee and making a face from it being very strong. "I keep having the same nightmare over and over again."

"You know how the old man is about those things," Phillip said. "Besides, you keep dreaming that and it could be a premonition or come true."

"I would if I could," Paul said after another sip of coffee. "Besides, how do you know it hasn't already?"

"Well try and relax, we'll be in port soon and this will all be forgotten," Phillip said confidently.

"How can you be so sure?" Paul asked. "Doesn't it bother you that we have been sailing and haven't seen anything? No ships, no land, not even a seagull. We've been sailing in the same weather since the storm and not getting anywhere."

"You're beginning to sound delusional," Phillip countered. "People will think you're insane. We've been fortunate to have this weather since the storm. I almost thought we were goners."

"How do you know we weren't? Paul asked. "Honestly, how do we know we weren't?"

"Those dreams have really affected you, haven't they?" Phillip asked.

"Yes, they have," Paul admitted. "They are so vivid and real. There is something to them, I'm telling you."

Phillips facial expression changed from laid back to serious. "You really believe this don't you?" he asked.

"Yes," Paul admitted as he shifted forward in his chair. "There is something wrong here. I can feel it. I just can't figure it out."

"Well try not to let it bother you or think about it too much?" Phillip asked. "You're just shook up from that storm is all. I don't blame you it was a pretty bad one. It even got to me some."

"That's easier said than done," Paul replied. "I feel like ever since we went through the storm we've been sailing in from forever to eternity and back again."

"Relax," Phillip said trying to reassure his friend. "The old man would rather be damned than see his precious ship sink. He'd sell his soul first. He'll make sure we get to our destination."

Paul shook his head. The phrase about the captain being damned and selling his soul sent a chill through him. He tried to mutter something but could not. All he could say was "Maybe."

"Well, I have to get back," Phillip said, standing up. "I was just making my rounds." He then placed his hand on Paul's. It felt ice cold.

"Phillip, your hands are ice cold,' Paul said, surprised.

"Yeah, well you know cold hands, warm heart," Phillip joked before leaving the galley.

Phillip's cold hands disturbed Paul more than his earlier comment. Paul then noticed that the table in front of where Paul had been sitting was wet. He touched it and found it cold as well.

When Paul stood up, he noticed that the chair Phillip had been seated in was wet as well. Paul finished his coffee and left the galley.

As Paul made his way below deck, he could not help but notice how cold and wet looking it appeared to be. Even the crew appeared pale and different. He just wasn't sure why and what it was. He had trouble trusting his own senses.

Paul returned to his duties on deck, but with much

more trepidation and doubt.

"Glad you could finally join us, Mr. Landon," Captain Vanderdecker said. "Did your sustenance change your outlook any?"

"Sir?"

"I asked if your sustenance changed your outlook," the captain repeated his question.

"I don't know," Paul replied.

"You don't know?" Captain Vanderdecker yelled. "What in the hell do you mean by that? You're in the middle of a Great Lake. What else are you going to see except water?"

"But, Captain, we haven't seen anything since the storm," Paul weakly protested. "We haven't seen a ship, land or anything."

"It's near the end of the sailing year, Mr. Landon, so that is not unusual," Vanderdecker explained. "So, we are less apt to see anything this time of year. Does that answer your questions?"

"Yes, Sir," Paul replied, unconvincingly.

"Either way, I need to go below," Vanderdecker said. "I need you to take over."

"Yes, Sir,"

Paul watched as Captain Vanderdecker walked away. He thought it very odd and a bit uncanny that the captain did not appear to cast a shadow in the daylight. Then again, as he looked around nobody else did either. He looked down at the deck and also noticed that the captain left wet footprints behind him.

Paul closed his eyes and wondered if he were going insane. Whatever this madness was, he wanted it to end. He hoped they arrived at their destination soon for his own mental sake.

As he held the wheel, keeping the ship steady he observed the men working and interacting with each other. Upon his first glance, it seemed to so ordinary. But as he continued watching them, they continued doing the same things over and over again, as if stuck in a repetitive motion.

Paul wanted to scream but covered his mouth with his left hand as he was filled with horror.

Now he knew that he wasn't insane.

He knew something was horribly wrong.

Now he was certain that he wasn't insane and suffering from some kind of madness after all. He felt both relieved and terrified at the prospects.

The sum of his greatest fears was not only coming true, but already had and almost undeniable.

It wasn't death he feared, but being somewhere in between, stuck in a kind of an endless Purgatory of never-ending repetition where every day was the exact same one.

Tears filled his eyes as he realized how they were all doomed.

For one of the few times in his life, Paul was frightened and did not know what to do.

He tried not to watch the crew, but that was futile. Scanning the horizon offered him little comfort in that the sky and water remained constant and unchanging. Just like the ship and the crew it stayed the same.

"*Hell is repetition*," he thought, fearfully.

After some time at the wheel, Captain Vanderdecker and Phillip returned.

Paul knew he had to tell them of his discovery.

"Captain! Phillip!" he announced. "I know what is wrong! I've figured it out! We're all dead! We must have gone down during the storm that I've been dreaming about!"

Captain Vanderdecker and Phillip exchanged looks. The rest of the crew silently and gradually moved in behind them.

Finally, after a long silent pause Phillip spoke. "Well of course we are!" he exclaimed with a wicked smile.

"Not only that, Mr. Landon," Captain Vanderdecker added. "We are damned!"

As Paul looked at all of their faces, he saw them as pale, lifeless beings who looked as if they had drowned. He let out a blood-curdling scream as they moved in, swarming him. Paul lost consciousness, mid-scream from the overwhelming horror of it all.

Paul Landon sat up in his bunk screaming out in terror and pain. He looked around realizing that he was in his cabin aboard his ship. As he wiped away the sweat from his brow, he realized that he had another nightmare and any thought of trying to get any sleep an exercise in futility.

"Dear, God not again," he moaned, still shaking from the horrible dream. "Not again, please, not again."

There was a knock on his cabin door, and it opened. "Are you alright, Sir," asked crewman Chester Blakeslee.

"Yeah, I'm alright," Paul groaned in return.

"Another bad dream?" Chester asked.

"Yeah," Paul replied. "The same damn one."

Time to Pay the Piper

I am the last one.

The last surviving child from the Hamlenburg Village tragedy of 1936.

With the death of my longtime and childhood friend Peter Hagan last week and the death of my other friend Beverly Willis five years ago, I am all that is left from the children that lived in town then.

I remember it as if it were yesterday. The memories are still that vivid. Now and then I still have nightmares about it. Even after all of these years it still seems unbelievable.

It all started in the summer of 1936. Hamlenburg Village was a small farming community towards the east side of northern lower Michigan. It was made up of a number of families of Germanic and Northwest European ancestry. It had been a great place to live and grow up.

At least until that summer

After a very hard and cold winter we had a long dry spell with no rain. Farmers were getting concerned. Rainfall was well below what was needed to sustain the crops and people were terrified at the prospect of becoming like the "dustbowl" areas out west like in Oklahoma. On top of that the heat was almost unbearable.

As kids we didn't notice that much, but four elderly people had succumbed to the heat and a couple of others had heat stroke. Some were friends and neighbors of ours. Old Mr. Latimer wasn't seen for days until someone noticed a foul smell coming from his house. By the time they found him he was all bloated up like the Michelin

Man in his white long johns sitting in his easy chair. From what I heard the first ones to find him became physically sick and he had to be buried right away on his own property.

Anyway, nothing was growing. It was almost like a drought and people were getting pretty desperate.

Then one day he came to town.

Wolfgang Teuful.

He was a golden haired, handsome man with clear blue eyes, friendly smile and crisp brown uniform. He was cultured, polite and from the old country. He appeared to be a man of wealth and property. Most importantly, he appeared to have a solution to the farmers' dilemma

All of the ladies from 16 to 60 swooned over him. Even most of the men seemed in awe of him. Too many, he appeared almost angelic.

We would later find out that he had received a letter from Konrad Becker, a German-American Volksbund member, of which half the town were also members that he decided to offer some help. Becker was also one of the elderly people who succumbed to the heat almost immediately after he had sent the letter.

Anyway, Teuful came to town and headed immediately to the town hall where he approached the town council about possibility of helping the community. They were receptive to any offer of assistance. That was how desperate things were. The next Sunday in both the Lutheran and Catholic churches in town, it was announced that there would be a town hall meeting on Wednesday at seven p.m.

Almost the whole community showed up. I had a front row seat with my parents and older brother and sister Max, and Mila. I noticed immediately how Max wanted to be like him and how Mila seemed to just adore him.

Josef Hostettler, the head of the town council introduced Teuful. He said this man had come to town offering help to our current crisis.

Teuful took to the podium. Tall, and handsome, he looked so regal. He thanked everybody for coming and said he was there to offer some assistance from the Fatherland to our plight. He mentioned how he received a letter from Mr. Becker and that convinced him and his superiors to see what they could do.

He said he had some scientifically modified German seed and fertilizer to help boost our crops growth and output. In fact, he said that he expected the corn and wheat to be at least knee high by the Fourth of July.

There was a lot of mumbling and murmurs of disbelief, but he held his hands up like a priest and said, he understood our doubts, but he was prepared show us how.

Mr. Jacob Fischer asked what this all would cost. A few others echoed his sentiments, saying help like this did not come free.

Other than that, only two really had any serious doubts. One was the local newspaperman John Klein and the other was our schoolteacher Ernestine Bonner. They were the only two with questions and any serious reservations about it.

Teuful smiled and nodded. He said there would be no financial cost. He then offered the deal of a proper education for Hamlenburg's children back in the Fatherland, at no cost to the community. He added that it would be like studying abroad so that their children could come back better equipped to handle problems like this in the future. He offered to help prepare them for this after church for a couple hours each Sunday. He said there was one caveat in there would be physicals and some set standards for them to pass for this to happen.

He said they would be part of a better future.

There were more murmurs and private discussions in the audience.

Teuful then spoke up, offering to pay for a large Fourth of July picnic for the entire community in a few weeks. In the meantime, if the farmers did not mind, he would like to get started on helping them out.

Pretty much everybody agreed that something needed to be done, even my parents agreed. So, it was then voted on and passed. The only holdouts were Bonner and Fletcher.

Afterwards everybody went up and shook Teuful's hand, thanking him. It was then that I noticed that along with my sister, two other girls Heidi Hein and Erika Schmidt both were also equally enamored with Teuful.

That week the first shipments of seed and fertilizer were delivered to all of the farms. I was helping my dad and Max as much as I could. I had just broken leg after falling out of a hay loft. Anyway, as we were spreading it Max and I found what looked like a finger bone. Dad said it was unfortunate but was probably mixed in after a horrible accident. We didn't think anything of it at the time. Later we would find out others had found similar things like that in their fertilizer as well.

That next Sunday Teuful began his tutelage of about two dozen young people between 12-17. They were all my friends and neighbors.

Just before the picnic arrived Miss Bonner was found dead. The rumor was that she fell down the stairs in her house and broke her neck. Someone theorized that she tripped over one of her cats and lost her balance.

John Klein wasn't so sure. He always had doubts. He had heard tales of body parts being found in the fertilizer. He was suspicious of Teuful from the beginning. There was something he did not trust about him.

Teuful had been right. The corn, wheat and other

crops were at least knee high by the first of July. Everybody was almost euphoric. Teuful was invited to several families' Sunday dinners. He had truly ingratiated himself to the community. Especially the kids he was preparing and mentoring. My own brother and sister included.

By the time the picnic rolled around we heard that Heidi Hein had killed herself. There were all kinds of hushed talk and rumors. I overheard my parents talking and they said she was pregnant. Suspicions immediately fell upon her boyfriend Peter Schmidt. Her father physically attacked him and then tried to shoot him but was restrained before doing so. But even he was shocked by her death. He said that Heidi had acted differently towards him ever since Teuful arrived. In fact, she had spent a lot of time with him. She no longer wanted to be seen with him. Needless to say, he was forced to leave town due to the gossip and perception.

We knew he left broken-hearted.

As the crops continued to grow and flourish, Teuful became more and more popular. As his popularity grew, John Klein's declined. Nobody cared about his reservations and tough questions. He was ridiculed and cursed. A long-time friend and confidant of many in the community was viewed as a troublemaker and outsider. A couple of times he was almost assaulted by those who defended Wolfgang Teuful.

Then in early August a mysterious fire broke out at the newspaper. When John Klein tried to put out the fire he was beaten up by several assailants. That was pretty much the end of John Klein. Like Peter Schmidt he soon left town. There was nothing else to keep him there.

I remember the last words he used in his last newspaper editorial. They were also his parting words to a few people still friendly to him. Klein asked. "What have we wrought? Has anybody asked that question? We sold our souls for what could be a temporary situation. What will you do when it comes time to pay the piper? What will the price be? Can you afford it?"

Nobody could answer his questions. He said goodbye and those few people bid him farewell.

Though I didn't understand at the time, I never forgot that.

I'm not sure what happened to him after that. I never really bothered to find out.

About the same time, Teuful was gaining in prominence and popularity.

Just before harvest time Erika Schmidt was found drowned in the nearby pond where we went swimming. Most figured it was just a horrible accident. There was a rumor that she too was pregnant. Some thought it was a suicide.

In the meantime, Teuful's hold on the children of the Hamlenburg Village had grown immensely. Max wanted to be like him, and Mila was in love with him. From what I could tell at my young age the other twenty plus kids twelve and up were the same way. They were under his control.

In a way we all were. He was friendly, kind and very persuasive.

A couple of days before the harvest I was finally out of my cast. I had a noticeable limp and my leg strength was not where it should have been. The doctor said I may have the limp for the rest of my life. I went for a walk and ended up down near a stream.

I sat down in my tree fort that I had built with my friends, hidden away from view. It was then I saw Mila and Teuful together. They were not just together. They were together naked. I was in shock. I had never seen a naked girl before, let alone my sister. Or a naked man. I watched as Teuful was on top of my sister, grunting and growling like a possessed animal with his lean sinewy body thrusting into her.

I thought he was hurting her at first with her moaning and was going to help her, but then I saw her kiss him several times. It was then I realized she was really enjoying this. She wanted this. It was very apparent that she desired him, badly.

Even more shocking was afterwards as he got up and stood over her like a Greek god, she slid over on her knees and began to perform oral sex on him, as he pushed her head further onto himself. All the while he was laughing with evil delight as she continued to satisfy him.

I was shocked and surprised that my sister was doing this. It was disturbing. For a moment, I thought he looked like some kind of bronze-skinned monster as the sunlight glistened off his lean, sinewy perspiring body.

I turned away, crying and felt dirty for a long time afterward having witnessed this event. I stayed hidden until after I knew they were gone and went back home.

It was then that I realized that he wasn't some kind of helpful, Aryan angel sent from the Fatherland, but some kind of Nazi demon from Hell.

My leg hurt from all of the exertion and I did not sleep well that night.

That was when I realized there was something very wrong with Teuful. I began to wonder if I was the only one. I had grown distant from my friends who now idolized Teuful. To them, he was like a combination of Santa Claus, Superman and Jesus.

The next couple of weeks leading up to the harvest were a blur for me. So much was going on that nobody noticed how I was affected by what I had witnessed.

It was then that I began to get closer to Peter Hagen and Beverly Willis. Peter had lost his hearing after contacting pneumatic fever four years ago. For some reason or another we had drifted apart. I had also began talking to Beverly more as well. This helped me.

Now, the three of us were bonding because we were overlooked. Basically, because of our infirmities, we were ignored by Teuful.

He had no use for us.

While blind, Beverly could sense something about Teuful. Peter told us how he reminded him of a tiger or a leopard. Pretty, but very dangerous.

All the three of us could do was watch, and in Beverly's case listen as events continued.

Finally harvest time arrived. Everybody was busy. In spite of the weather and the conditions, the crops were plentiful. Teuful offered to provide beer and entertainment for a harvest time celebration. So, Labor Day weekend there was to be a celebration with a dance and a bonfire on Saturday night. Everybody was happy and excited.

The most excited were the kids that Teuful had been mentoring. They were planning and ready to go to Germany with him to continue their education. This was to be their celebration and farewell party as well.

There was one problem.

Many of the same parents who benefitted from Teuful's help were now hesitant to let their children accompany him to Germany, even with the promise of free education. Even my own parents were now hesitant for one reason or another. A few were alright with it and thought it would a good thing. But there were also the diehard Bundists who had a deep Aryan pride and ties to the Fatherland.

We had heard that some of kids that Teuful tutored were very upset and frustrated over this. He calmed them down and reminded them to respect their parent's wishes.

He calmly told the parents that he understood their reservations and wishes. This seemed to placate them.

He said there was no reason for any of this to dampen the harvest celebration.

Labor Day weekend arrived. With it came all of the merriment and all the festivities that were promised. It was great fun. It had been the first time I felt this way since before witnessing that incident with my sister and Teuful.

Many of the parents joined the kids as they held hands, danced and sang happy songs around the huge bonfire. Everybody appeared truly happy and grateful. I even enjoyed watching it. I think it was the most fun that Hamlenburg Village ever had.

Everybody was grateful to Teuful for what he had done for town.

Sometime after midnight it was announced that Teuful and the kids would clean up and make sure the bonfire was safely extinguished. Because he had built up such trust with the town, nobody thought much about it. So, when the celebration ended, and all of the adults went home Teuful and the kids were left to clean up.

That was where the Hamlenburg Village tragedy began.

I was awakened at five a.m. by my parents. It turns out my older brother and sister had not come home. I was asked if I knew anything. I replied that I did not. A few minutes later that our nearest neighbors Frederick and Lilith Krueger arrived. They told us how some twenty-four children between ages 12 and 17 had left with Wolfgang Teuful.

The Krueger's own sons Peter, Paul and Philip had gone as well.

They named off basically all of the kids between those ages that were now gone. On top of that Irwin Rieger and Max Krein were found dead.

No, not dead.

Murdered.

From what I had heard their bodies were macabre sight, laid out in the shape of a swastika. It turns out Teuful had not found them acceptable. Rieger and Krein both had Jewish lineage.

Teuful had disappeared with the kids like a thief in the night. Taking with him their most important possessions.

Their children.

There was a pall over the town after that.

There was only Peter, Beverly and I left in town. Plus a few babies that were only a few months old. Sadly, after all of this we were now we were finally cherished more than we had been.

Sometime later my parents received pictures of Max and Mila from Germany. Max was part of the Hitlerjugend or Hitler Youth. He was a group leader. We figured Mila had gotten pregnant by Teuful and had a son, Wolfgang. I had finally told my parents about what I had witnessed earlier.

It turns out some of the other parents received a few periodic updates as well. Many had sent goodbye letters saying they thought of the Fuhrer as their Father and that was where their loyalties would now lie.

Each year, for about eight years we would somehow continue to receive pictures of Mila with her growing brood of offspring with Teuful. By 1944 she had six children, four boys and two girls. Mila was killed during one of the allied bombings of Germany. We do not know what happened to her children.

Max made Lieutenant and was awarded the Iron Cross. We heard later that he was killed somewhere in France just after the Normandy Invasion.

They were two of the few we were able to find out anything on. Eventually the people in our town contacted our congressman to see what he could find out about the others. Hamlenburg Village residents were eventually contacted individually by some government representatives with information about their children. Because the Germans were meticulous record keepers, the information was not long in coming.

My brother and sister were not the only ones who died there. The Krueger triplets were all lost on the Russian front at different times.

Eventually word trickled out what had happened to the others that Teuful had taken with him. Every single one of them had died or been killed.

We eventually found out that Arthur and Jacob Hess, Hermann Hein, Walter Lang, William Kohl, and Albert Bauer were all killed or died somewhere near or around the times between Stalingrad and Kursk.

Christian Becker, Frederick Encke and Louis Meyer were missing in action and presumed dead during the war.

Josef Wagner was alive, but in a mental hospital. He had lost three of his limbs and was a victim of severe shell shock. Mentally insane, he was another lost soul. He died sometime in 1947.

As for the girls that left, we heard that Elsa Kalt, Lisa Steiner, Elisabeth Fischer and Maria Hodel were said to have been killed during the firebombing of Dresden. They, like my sister were supposedly mothers with children too. Nobody knows much of what happened to their offspring either.

Heidi Mueller, Eva Beck and Hilda Sager died or committed suicide while trying to defend Berlin from the invading Russian army.

Elisabeth Fischer's sister Ingrid died in childbirth either before or early in the war. She was the only one who died relatively in a peaceful way.

John Klein's parting words had echoed in my head. Our town had finally paid the piper and it had been much too costly.

After the war, the town referred to the loss of the children as the Hamlenburg Village tragedy. The town had a service every year to place wreaths and flowers on cemetery markers that commemorated the deaths of the children. Many of the parents were not the same after that.

Some died shortly after the war. My mother died in 1946 at 45. My dad sold the farm two years later and ended up working at a nearby feed store. He used some of the money towards my college. I ended up becoming a veterinarian.

As for Peter, Beverly and myself we stayed close. Peter eventually went on to a special school and ended up doing pioneering research in deafness and hearing disabilities. He married a classmate and they had a son. Beverly met and married a paratrooper after the war. They ended up having four kids. As for me, I eventually moved out of Hamlenburg, married and had kids of my own.

Every year until about ten years ago we got together to have dinner and toast those that we knew and lost, thankful for our long and enduring friendship.

As for Teuful nobody heard of him or what had happened to him. He disappeared like a lot of Nazis after that. Some speculated that they were not even sure he was a man at all, but some kind of devil or demon. Even the allies had not heard of him or even knew who he was. We had heard a few other men like him came to the country to recruit the flower of German-American citizens and bring them back to Germany to take part in some kind of New World Order.

There was speculation some time ago that he was in Argentina with his kids and the surviving children of

Hamlenburg Village kids. But that was just rumor and many years ago. He has to be dead by now. We eventually found out Wolfgang Teuful's name meant basically "Wolf" and "Diabolic" or "Devil."

Whoever Wolfgang Teuful was, he was a kind of handsome, blonde-haired, blue-eyed Pied-Piper from Hell.

All he did was lead them down the path to death and destruction with his golden words that were music to the ears of those young and naive enough to believe them. Instead of following Teuful into a brighter future, he led them into graveyard with the Devil's evil tune.

Singing the song of death and destruction.

The Best Laid Plans

The months of preparation and planning for every contingency had finally come to an end. Now it was time for the execution of these plans that had been so thoroughly overseen and poured over for so many hours, days and months.

For Ahmed Jarrah this had been the culmination of an idea that had begun over a year ago. He was wholly satisfied that all of the planning and possible contingencies had been covered and planned for. Once again, it just boiled down to executing these plans.

He watched patiently as the special package that he had smuggled made its way via an accomplice towards the luggage carrier that was to be loaded into a 747 at London's Heathrow Airport. He had done his part, packing the leather suitcase with plastic explosives and a timer that was set to explode an hour into the plane's flight.

Jarrah felt a great sense of satisfaction about it all. He had been the chief architect and planner of this particular mission. It had been his hellish baby since its inception. So, like a proud father of a terrible baby, he stood filled with a prideful kind of excitement and anticipation for it to be a big success.

The twenty-nine-year-old, Saudi Arabian man was for all intents and purposes an assassin of sort by trade. Officially he was a chemical engineer. Clandestinely he was a cold-blooded killer. Others referred to him as a terrorist, while he preferred to be thought of as a Jihadist or a warrior for Allah.

A somewhat handsome man with a neatly trimmed beard, Jarrah was radicalized at an early age. He was educated in the West in chemical engineering as well as to learn the language and their ways to make it easier to infiltrate their societies. By the time he was a teenager, Jarrah was proficient with an AK-47 and other weapons as well as being an excellent bomb maker.

He had been quite effective and proficient at the blowing up of airliners and buildings that in turn killed hundreds for his cause. The deaths of the innocents did not matter to him. To Jarrah, they were infidels and therefore unworthy of anything other than disdain and retribution.

He killed indiscriminately, while playing the part of a peace-loving diplomatic type hoping for peace and friendship throughout the world. Deep down he was a cold-blooded killer, wanting to spread Jihad throughout the world.

Now Jarrah waited patiently in the terminal after handing off his special package of plastic explosives and other combustible materials to destroy the airliner. His plan was to destroy some members of the Royal Family that were supposed to be heading to New York.

The intelligence that they gathered over the last several months had given Jarrah and his fellow accomplices every indication that they were using this airliner for their trip and at this particular time. So, Jarrah's terrorist cell planned accordingly in trying to match up their plan with the Royal Family's itinerary.

Now he just had to hope his contact in the ground crew, Mohammed Shabazz, did his job thoroughly and accurately, especially in placing the bomb near the 747's fuel tank.

All he could do was watch and wait.

As he waited, he began to reminisce about his other

successful acts of terrorism. Each of his other success had led to his planning of this one. His confidence had grown as such to plan something much bigger.

This had been it.

Deal a deadly blow to the Royal Family. It didn't really which members of the family it was. While the queen and her husband would have been the biggest target, her offspring, grandchildren and great-grandchildren would be just as good. Either way it would strike at the core of Great Britain. Especially since they had sided with that Great Satan, the United States of America and Israel, against him and his allies.

This particular plan, when successful, would make all of the others appear small and insignificant by comparison. Before, it had been a bunch of nameless victims, this would be people known the world over. Not even the terrorists on 9/11 could make that claim, even if they did manage to kill thousands and destroy the World Trade Center.

This would be a new precedent as far as Jarrah was concerned.

A new horrific one.

The very thought of this pleased him very much.

It would especially please his comrades in arms and allies in their quest for global Jihad.

Jarrah thought that he had planned for every contingency. No matter how small or how large, he had an answer for them. Nothing was going to stop his plan now as far as he could see.

Now he just had to wait for members of the Royal Family to leave.

None of his family or himself would be suspect since they were touring Europe and England as well.

Jarrah's own family was prepared to leave London as well. They would be departing later for Riyadh, Saudi

Arabia. His parents, siblings and their spouses, cousins, nieces and nephews and his own pregnant wife were leaving after touring Europe. London was their last stop.

Jarrah would fly back on a later flight to join up with them. He had to see his mission through and would be unable to leave with them at that time. Plus, if there was a chance that he was caught, he did not want his family implicated.

It was all for the best.

He just hoped that his contact Mohammed Shabazz did not get caught or accidently detonate the bomb. There was always that possibility, but Shabazz was a smart and dedicated warrior like he was, so he did not think so.

While not college educated like Jarrah, Shabazz also came from a very-well-off family. While Jarrah's family was a wealthy one, Shabbazz's family was not left for wanting of much either, even though they were not as rich.

Shabazz wheeled the over-sized cart towards the area where the luggage was to be taken to be loaded onto that particular flight. He made sure to place Jarrah's suitcase right in the middle and on top of the pile of bags and suitcases.

Shabazz momentarily parked his cart next to another that was bound for Frankfurt, Germany. Knowing they would be loading the cart onto the plane soon, Shabazz decided that he had time to use the bathroom. He felt it was safe to do so since there was nobody else around at the time. Besides, he had to urinate very badly and could not hold it anymore.

Once Shabazz had entered the bathroom, another ground crewman, Keith Jones, had trouble pushing his luggage cart. The wheels swiveled all over the place and it did not move right. It was long overdue for repair, but they were momentarily short.

"Who in the bloody Hell decided this bloody cart was alright to use?" Jones thought as he fought vainly to push the cart towards the holding area.

After struggling with it, he lost control of his own overloaded cart and it crashed into the luggage cart Shabazz had been pushing earlier. The baggage flew off of both, crashing and tumbling all over the floor in large piles.

"Bullocks!" Jones cursed, knowing that he would have to sort the suitcases and bags before reloading the carts by himself. "Bullocks! Bloody Hell! Bullocks!"

Jones picked up most of the luggage and bags by himself. By the time Shabazz returned from the bathroom, he found Jones placing the bags back onto both carts.

"What are you doing?" Shabazz asked.

"We had a little accident," Jones explained. "My cart has a bad wheel and crashed into your cart."

"Son-of-a-pig," Shabazz muttered under his breath and began to help pick up the remaining suitcases and bags.

Shabazz came across one that looked like the one Jarrah had handed him earlier. Without hesitation or even looking, he placed the suitcase back on the cart. Jones placed a similar one on the cart marked for New York. Finally, after a few minutes, the luggage was all put back in place.

Shabazz walked away. He turned back to make sure the "special" suitcase that Jarrah had given him was on the right cart. As he looked, he thought that he caught view of an identical looking suitcase on a flight bound for Riyadh. Shabazz started to walk away, then shook his head and looked back. The one cart had been rolled away to the jet bound for Saudi Arabia, while the other had been taken to the flight leaving for New York. He did not realize there were two identical suitcases when he placed the one back on the cart. He didn't really look at the tags of the one he placed on the cart. He wondered if Jones had read the tag when he placed the suitcase back on the other cart.

He began to have doubts as to whether he had placed the correct bag on the right flight. At first, he was certain that he had. Then he wasn't so sure. Then Shabazz convinced himself that he'd placed the correct one in its rightful place. He knew that to go back now would immediately draw some kind of suspicion on him and they might end up checking the bags.

Still, Shabazz was continued with doubts. He hoped that his mission had been accomplished but if he had not, Jarrah would be angry. But he knew it was too late now.

Either way, Jarrah's bomb would kill some infidels flying somewhere, even if he did not kill any of the Royals. He felt that he had done his job to the best of his ability and there was nothing more that he could do.

Meanwhile, Jarrah was with his family as they were about to leave. He'd traveled a similar route and joined them at times during their European trip. This had been his cover to do his nefarious and clandestine activities. As they began to board their flight, he said goodbye to his parents, wife, siblings, aunts, uncles and cousins. It was a warm and festive occasion for Jarrah's family.

"Is it done?" asked Jarrah's brother Amir.

Jarrah nodded. "Yes," he replied, confidently. "Now, we just have to wait.

Amir nodded. "Good," he muttered softly. "This will be epic, as they say."

"Definitely," Jarrah replied.

"We will see you in Riyadh," Jarrah's other brother, Abdullah, asked. "Right?"

Jarrah nodded. "Tomorrow at the latest," he replied. "I need to stay little longer. Just to make sure the plan was properly executed."

"We will toast your latest success at home," Amir said. "We will have a big celebration when you join us."

"Yes," Abdullah agreed. "It will be a glorious success. I know it. This will destroy the evil in world."

Jarrah nodded. "Yes," he hissed, with hope and excitement. "It shall be. Nothing is going to stop it now. Members of the Royal Family will die. We shall vanquish some of the evil that exists today."

Jarrah's brothers smiled and laughed. They were young and jubilant about their brother's forthcoming success.

"We shall get the family home first," Amir announced. "You take care and be careful. They will be looking for you. Do what you have to do. Just be careful. Be sure to cover your tracks and hide amongst the cells throughout this country."

"I shall," Jarrah said. "I have a place located in a Muslim section of London. There are many like us there and I can blend in and hide. Besides, the English are very stupid and slow on this."

"Outstanding," Amir commented. "You seem to have thought of everything."

"I hope so," Jarrah replied. "I also have fake passports. If worse comes to worse, I will take the Chunnel or a boat to France and leave by flight for there."

"I wish I had your ability to plan like this," Abdullah admitted. "Is he not a genius?"

"Yes, he is," Amir agreed. "Our whole family is proud of you. Your name shall live in infamy in our family for eternity."

"Yes," Abdullah agreed. "None have ever been so cunning and smart as him."

"I don't know about that," Jarrah replied, humbly. "I am but a humble warrior for Allah."

"Allah be praise by your faithfulness," Amir

commented.

"Allah be with you," Abdullah said, before hugging his brother.

"And to you as well," Jarrah said, hugging him back.

Amir hugged his brother. "You are why we shall win this battle," he stated.

Jarrah nodded. "Be safe my brothers," he said. "See you soon."

Both of Jarrah's brothers nodded and then waved before they silently followed the rest of the family on their way to board the plane. Jarrah watched the long procession of his family leave as the last call for Flight 51 came over the airport loudspeaker. He was both happy and sad to see the all go.

At that time, Jarrah never felt such love for his family as he did at that time. He took a deep breath and exhaled. He felt a great sense of pride and exhilaration inside him. All of his planning and perseverance were about to pay off big time and he knew it.

He could feel it building up to a grand finale.

Now, he just had to wait. It was all a matter of time.

Jarrah decided to head to his apartment in London. It was a small place, located in a densely populated Muslim area. It was also perfect for him to sit back and wait for events to unfold. He knew that he was amongst friends and allies there and felt safe. He knew that if needed they would hide him at moment's notice. On his way back to his apartment, he picked up a Halal meal to eat before watching the news unfold before him.

Once home, Jarrah got down and prayed Eastward towards Mecca. Once he had finished, Jarrah then placed his meal on the table in front of him and began to eat. He used the television remote to turn on the T.V. and flipped through the channels.

"Western television is shit," he muttered to himself as

he continued to flip through the channels before finally settling on the BBC channel.

He waited with baited-breath and listened to the BBC's nightly report.

The first report that caught his attention was that the Royal Family had postponed their trip to New York and decided to take holiday at Balmoral Castle to celebrate some special event that he did not hear since, Jarrah stopped listening when they were not on the flight. Deeply disappointed, he was upset and wondered who was on the plane with the bomb, if it wasn't them. He had wasted so much time planning to do this, and now it was all shot to Hell.

They had not even been on the plane.

He had failed.

His only consolation was that some other evil people would die instead. Possibly more infidels to his growing list of victims. Jarrah thought that would have to do for now. He would have to plan again for the next opportunity.

As he ate his meal, he continued to watch the news. There was a special report that came on, announcing that a 747 out of Heathrow Airport had exploded over the Italian Alps. He listened intently with a large smile on his face. At least his bomb was not a total waste.

He was riding a little higher than he had been earlier. Jarrah still pumped his fist in the air in jubilation over having killed some more people that he deemed were unworthy.

Then he caught something that the newscaster said during his momentary celebration and listened intently. The reporter repeated that the 747 was flight 51 out of Heathrow Airport that was headed for Riyadh, Saudi Arabia, killing everybody on board. They reported that terrorism was strongly suspected, and searchers were trying to reach the area where most of the plane went down.

Jarrah's jaw hit the floor in shock and disbelief. With the exception of only a few older and sickly relatives in Saudi Arabia, Jarrah's entire family had just been killed. He felt sick in the pit of his stomach as tears streamed down his cheeks.

He was devastated.

Finally, he cried out in personal pain and anguish. "No!!!" he then fell to the floor, sobbing uncontrollably. *"How could this have happened?"* he thought.

Jarrah remembered all of the things his brothers had said to him, all of which now proved to be untrue and unfounded. He was none of those things because of the catastrophic failure on his part.

Jarrah fell to his knees on the floor, wailing in pain and despair like an animal caught in a trap, a trap of his own design and making. In his inconsolable, heartbroken and tear-filled rambling, Jarrah damned Shabazz for his terrible mistake. After a few minutes, he calmed down enough to where he was only sobbing.

Jarrah was now starting to become angry. Where the hell was Shabazz, he wondered, and what did he do? After a few minutes he was finally able to muster the strength to get off the floor. He sat back down on the couch, with tears streaming down his cheeks. "How?" he asked, hoarsely "How?"

He then grabbed a pistol from on top of his dresser and sat back down on his couch. He was planning to use it on Shabazz.

Meanwhile, Shabazz had also heard the news while still at work. The uncertainty and doubts of earlier had come to fruition. He had made a very costly mistake, one that became a very deadly one. One that not only would haunt him, but possibly lead to back to him as well. He was filled with terror. He knew he was now a dead man walking. He knew that not only Jarrah would be after him for this egregious mistake, but Scotland Yard and other intelligences services as well.

He knew there was no escape.

Save one.

And that was not really and escape at all. But it was his only solution.

Shabazz knew what he had to do.

Shabazz prayed, found some rope in the supply area. He then took it to the employee men's bathroom in the shipping area. After that he then got a small step ladder, tied a loop in it the cord, placed his neck in the loop, kicked away the step ladder and hung himself.

Death could not come fast enough for him.

He would forever be known and feel the shame of being an abject failure by friend and foe alike.

Ironically, it was Keith Jones who would find him hanging from a pipe in the ceiling of the men's bathroom

After regaining himself enough to listen, Jarrah was able to listen to the BBC broadcast a short time later reporting that an airport worker named Mohammed Shabazz was found dead by an apparent suicide at the airport shipping area restroom. Authorities were still speculating whether there was a connection between his death and the airliner blowing up.

For all of Ahmed Jarrah's best laid plans had fallen to pieces and like the plane his family was on blew up in his face, costing him everything that mattered most in his life. Worst of all, he was to blame for all of it and he knew it.

In his quest to deal out death to others, he dealt it to his own family first.

Now, he sat numb and immobilized while sobbing on his couch. He heard sirens of the authorities getting louder and closer. He knew they were closing in on him. They had somehow figured it all out. Jarrah heard them stop outside his building as he raised the pistol to his head.

As a dealer in death, this was his only future.

Sufletul Mortii

It was an artistic piece of sinister beauty, a portrait that was painted in the colors of blood, evil, malevolence, and death. Speaking of futures past and of times not yet conceived or dreamt of.

It was timeless.

Darkness emanated from it. Yet it seduced the eyes that beheld it.

It went by many descriptions, all of them the same in its many trails and journeys throughout the ages and its temporary destinations.

Even the portrait's name, *Sufletul Mortii*, Romanian for *Soul Eater*, echoed its dark nature.

And it bore witness to history.

To kings and tyrants—war, famine, death and destruction. It was present to it all, getting richer and more vivid in color with each tragedy.

It brought forth ruin and death to all who possessed it. The portrait could never be owned, only purchased for a time. In turn, it owned a piece of each person that beheld it.

No artist was ever known, though many speculated it was painted by the Devil himself, with the blood and souls of man. It yearned to be found and admired. It wasn't particular to who its admirers were. It could entrance almost anyone.

We came across it quite by accident. We sought shelter in a decrepit, old monastery from a tumultuous storm during our trip across Europe. They heavy rains had washed out the bridge to the town ahead; a large tree had become uprooted and blocked the road behind us.

While aged and dilapidated, there still remained a few wooden benches, chairs, and pews.

We called out to announce our presence.

There was no answer.

As the storm raged outside, we became acclimated to our new but temporary surroundings and began to explore the place.

Cautiously, we opened doors to other rooms long since deserted and only host to memories and ghosts.

Constance and Veronica clung to us closely for protection and reassurance. While there were no signs of occupancy, we didn't feel alone. There was a darkness present other than the mid-day storm that interrupted our journey.

At last we explored a back room and cellar area. It was there in the back room that we found what would be the source of our worst nightmares.

We opened the door, and the first thing that caught our attention was the enormous life-size oval portrait on the wall.

Upon seeing it, Constance screamed.

Its image was so life-like and visceral.

It was perhaps the most disturbing piece of artwork I had ever been witness to.

What we beheld was a portrait that was filled with and radiated evil. No. It *was* evil, unlike any kind I had ever seen. We stood before it, studying it, as it hung there studying us in return. It felt like it was boring into our souls.

My friend, Peter, commented that it was sinister. Mesmerizing. Horrid yet enticing.

I don't remember how much time we spent entranced by it. The portrait seemed so horrifyingly real we could hardly move.

I finally found the strength to turn away.

It was then I noticed in a large chair, the skeletal remains of what had once been a priest. He, or rather his skeleton, lay in his ceremonial robes. Next to him on the floor was an old, thick leather-bound book.

Constance and Peter turned around, and when she saw the robed corpse, she screamed. Her shock echoed in the empty monastery.

Yet her loud echoing scream had no effect on Veronica. It didn't even faze her as she kept staring at the portrait. I went over and picked up the book. As I opened it and turned the pages, I realized it was about the portrait.

We left, seeking the safer confines of the sanctuary. Peter had to grab Veronica and physically move her; she was so mesmerized by it.

Waiting for the storm to pass, I began to read aloud from the book. It was troublesome at times, trying to decipher the old and faded Edwardian script. But I finally managed:

"The portrait was commissioned by Vlad Drakulya, later known as the infamous Vlad the Impaler. He desired a portrait to hang in the main hall of his castle. He demanded that the portrait be so terrifyingly real that it would instantly instill fear and horror amongst friend and foe alike."

I paused and looked at the others, uncertain until they nodded for me to continue:

"The artist, unknown only to Vlad, sent with it an emissary as a present. Vlad accepted the portrait with joy and gratitude. The emissary told Vlad that the portrait had been painted with the blood of his enemies. That it was worked in not only oils, but death, fear, and all the nightmares that existed with man."

I continued to read:

"Vlad cherished it. Ironically, Vlad would fall prey to its horror and malevolence as well."

Then I noticed the writing style changed. I couldn't make out the lettering, but it I guessed it looked as if it were written in Latin. I tried to read it but couldn't.

Some of the writing was too indistinguishable to read.

Finally, I came across another legible passage:

"The portrait, Sufletul Mortii, was given as a gift to Elizabeth Bathory, the Blood Countess of Hungary, on her twenty-first birthday."

"Who was Elizabeth Bathory?" Constance asked.

I continued to read:

"The portrait was hung in the room where legend states she murdered some six hundred and fifty victims. The portrait continued to hang in the sealed wing where the Countess remained in exile until her death."

I started to notice a trend with this huge oval portrait, the *Sufletul Mortii.* The portrait was always around death, destruction, bloodshed, and evil.

"Keep reading," Peter said.

"The portrait surfaced again in Germany during the Thirty Years War between the Catholics and the Lutherans. It was captured and taken to Charles the fifth of the Holy Roman Empire where it was hidden away. He could not stand the portrait, rumors indicated he feared it, and sent it to France—away from the Vatican."

I then came across more of the text in a language I couldn't name nor read, thus I was forced to skip ahead delving further into the book:

"The portrait became a gift to Louis the Sixteenth and was later handed down to Napoleon Bonaparte. Both men were in possession of the Sufletul Mortii unto their destruction and deaths."

An old blood stain smeared the handwriting over the next paragraph.

After a few moments I was finally able to decipher another section and started to read once again:

"It was in the possession of Archduke Franz Ferdinand of Austria. The Archduke's assassination was the catalyst that set off World War One."

I scanned the next paragraph, my eyes catching word of a name well known to history. I paused.

"What does the last paragraph say, Christopher?" Constance asked.

"When the Germans under the newly elected fuehrer reunified Austria as part of Germany, the German army took over and annexed the country. Kurt Schuschnigg, a Nazi sympathizing Austrian Chancellor, gave the portrait—the Sufletul Mortii—to his friend and ally the Fuhrer, Adolph Hitler."

There was no writing after that. We could only conclude it had been here ever since.

When I stopped reading, we noticed Veronica was gone. While I was reading from the book, the three of us had become distracted.

We immediately knew where she had gone.

An uncomfortable silence filled the room as a chill

went through us. Peter agreed to go and check on her, while Constance and I stayed in the sanctuary.

A few minutes later, we heard an ungodly scream, a mixture of sheer terror and gut-wrenching pain.

Fighting back fear, we headed towards the source of the scream. Peter was on the floor, on his knees sobbing like an inconsolable child. It was then we noticed Veronica. It was no longer her. Her clothes merely covered what was left of her skeletal remains. Constance shrieked.

I glanced at the portrait. Something about it had changed. It was already life-like, but now it seemed almost alive. I moved closer to it, being cautious, but kept what I thought was a safe distance. For a moment, I thought I could hear soft cries—distant and faint—coming from it. But then I reasoned my imagination was getting the best of me. Standing closer, I could sense the terrible darkness coming from the portrait. It had changed.

Its power had grown.

I knew we had to leave as soon as possible. Though I couldn't understand it, I knew we were in danger if we stayed here. Especially in the portrait room. Turning away, I thought I had heard a deep guttural sound, a kind of death growl.

I sensed that the portrait was the embodiment of evil. Alive and awaiting its next victim.

I told Constance to help me grab Peter and leave the room. The both of us helped Peter out of there.

Uncertain of what Peter had seen, it couldn't have been good. His body trembled as we led him out.

Back in the sanctuary, we sat down, trying to make sense of it all. I knew that we had to leave, but the storm was just too bad.

After a few minutes, Peter had regained his self-control. He began to tell us what happened, that he knew she was somehow mesmerized by the painting.

When he entered the room, he saw her standing there. As he walked towards her, he noticed a large, dark, shadowy presence that reached out towards her. It pulled out a translucent image of her spirit out of her physical body and pulled it into the painting.

He reached out to touch her body, and she shriveled before him, collapsing to the floor in a heap of clothed bones. It was then that we heard him scream.

I didn't doubt him, but I didn't know what to think either. I knew I didn't want to stay here, but the weather was dictating our present travel plans.

The raging storm caused the old monastery to shake and rattle. The lights inside were growing dimmer as the day had progressed and the storm grew worse. We looked around, managing to find a few old oil lamps. Even with the additional light, we weren't any more comfortable.

At least we were sheltered and dry.

Peter was adamant that the portrait was evil and needed to be destroyed. He was positive it was alive. He thought it fed off of misery and evil that existed with its former owners, like Vlad the Impaler, Elizabeth Bathory, and Adolph Hitler. It fed off them until they had outlived their usefulness.

It was like a cancerous abomination that just took over and changed those who had it. It was not witness to history but part of it, helping to influence it.

I told Peter I would help him destroy it. Once the storm passed, we could burn it with the oil lamps and leave this God-forsaken place. He agreed.

We sat and discussed what our options were. Peter was upset and pacing around. After a few minutes, Constance and I noticed he was missing.

Instinctively we both knew where he was. We had hoped he hadn't suffered the same fate as Victoria.

We found him outside the closed door to the room.

He raised his index finger to his lips indicating we needed to be quiet and pay attention. We both listened intently but heard nothing.

"You didn't hear that," Peter asked.

All three of us stood quietly, listening for whatever it was he'd heard, but we were only met with silence. Silence and the furious storm raging outside.

A look of defeated resignation spread across his face. While we believe he had heard something coming from the room, we feared whatever it had been was working hard to seriously unnerve him.

We tried in vain to get him to return with us, but he refused. He was obsessed with hearing whatever was coming from the room that held the portrait.

I feared for our lives and our sanity.

We wondered if this storm would ever subside enough to let us leave. In the course of just a few hours, we had lost one member of our group to some dark, diabolical force and another was gradually losing his mind.

I returned to the book, to see if there was any clue to what could help protect ourselves from its malicious evil. Meanwhile, Constance had gone off to check on the storm.

As I flipped through the pages, a separate piece of paper fell out. I quietly began to read:

To whomever is reading this, my name is Brother Frederick. I am a member of the Order of the Sacred Trust. I am alone now—the last one left. We were keepers of an abomination that was created ages ago. A portrait. The Sufletul Mortii, Romanian for Soul Eater. It's a portrait of evil. No! It's a portrait that is the very essence of evil.

Our order was created to be caretakers of the portrait. We dedicated our lives to this sole purpose. We believed that had we kept the Sufletul Mortii locked away and hidden, that it would keep the world safe. We were mistaken. Nothing can keep the world safe as long as there are admirers to behold its sick and wicked beauty.

It wasn't long after we secured the portrait that things began to go awry. The first to succumb to the portrait's evil was Brother Thaddeus. He heard noises in the cellar and fearing mice, went to investigate. When the rest of us arrived, we were horrified. All that was left of him was his skeletal remains on the floor.

The next to fall prey was Brother Andrew.

He performed an exorcism on the portrait, believing this would rid it of its evil. In the middle of the exorcism, we heard a loud crash. The portrait had fallen on him. The ornately detailed metal frame landed on him and broke his neck.

When we lifted the portrait off of him, Brother Edward and Brother Stuart cut their hands on the frame very badly. Both later developed some kind of blood infection and died after a lengthy and painful illness.

We long debated what to do about this evil. Brother Paul suggested that we bury it, but it was decided that it was too dangerous to touch. It had been buried before in its history and always seemed to quite literally resurface.

It seemed that any course of action we took towards the portrait resulted in some sort of repercussion that ended in death. We kept it hidden away, locked up, until we could come to a conclusion on the matter.

Others here also succumbed to the wickedness of the portrait. Brother Mattias suffered a heart attack after gazing at it for lengthy periods of time. Father Michael began to pound on the portrait in anger, until his hands were bloodied. His demise reminded me of the scene in Macbeth. When he couldn't wash the blood off his hands, he went insane. We found him hanging from a beam in his room.

Then it was Brother Clinton and Brother Paul. Brother Clinton attempted to burn the portrait with a torch, and I swear it was the Devil's breath that blew, setting him aflame. We stood in horror as he burned to death.

Brother Paul finally took an axe to the portrait several times. After having finished, he turned his back for a moment, and something from the portrait reached out and decapitated him.

Eventually thirteen of us would die over the years. After each death, the portrait seemed more vivid and powerful. Unfortunately, those in the church that knew of our oath had passed on, and so we were forgotten.

Finally, there was only me. The seriousness of the task kept me going all of these years. I knew it was too important to not continue. It was my duty. I had sworn an oath to God.

In my loneliness, especially on dark and chilly nights, I could feel and hear the portrait call out to me. Chiding me. Teasing me. It knew I was alone.

But I remained strong. I avoided the portrait room. It was the only way to stay safe and stay alive. Yet I grew to feeling ill as of late.

One day, just after my evening prayers, during a particularly bad storm, I thought I heard a crash. I grabbed this book and headed back to its room. As I reached for the door, it opened by itself.

The portrait, the Sufletul Mortii, was waiting for me.

I entered, sitting down in a chair at the back of the room. While I didn't stare directly at the portrait, I knew it was coming for me. Wanting me. Wanting me like a predator watching its prey.

I also realized I was dying. My time here was ending. I started to recite the prayers for exorcism, but my pain was too great, and I had to stop. I think I fainted. I woke up hours later, weaker than before. I performed my last rites, then I began to write this warning.

The portrait is alive. The darkness is come for me. I no longer have the strength to fight it. It is coming…

It's—

I didn't know what to think. Maybe these were the delusions of an old and lonely man? Yet I knew better. I didn't know what to believe. I could only go by what I had witnessed thus far. Deep down, though, I knew it to be true. It was all so unbelievable to comprehend.

A loud crash brought me out of my reverie.

Constance was missing.

I headed off to find her. The door to the portrait room was open. I dreaded entering but did without hesitation.

Instantly, I was greeted by a sight of pure revulsion.

The portrait had fallen on Peter, crushing him. His face was still frozen in terror.

I looked closely along the frame of the portrait. The metal was very sharp in the more ornate spots. It reminded me of a rose with its thorns, and I wondered if it had been deliberate in design. Remembering Brother Frederick's warning, I looked for something to lift the portrait off of Peter, fearing to touch it.

Constance let out a scream and then began to cry. I stood there, holding her, trying to calm and reassure her, but I was having little effect.

We left the portrait room, closing the door behind us. I started to look around for something that could help lift the portrait and found nothing. I hated to leave him like that, but I didn't want to touch that portrait, especially after what I had just read.

Now there was just the two of us.

Constance sat down in the corner and began to weep. We held each other, trying to comfort one another; baffled that less than a few hours before, we were a simple group of friends trekking through Europe. Soon she began kissing me and before I knew it, we were in throws of passion, making love. We had momentarily forgotten about the portrait, about Peter and Veronica.

We slept. I don't know for how long, but I woke up alone. The sanctuary felt icy and cold.

Constance was nowhere to be found. It was night,

and the worst of the storm had moved off in the distance.

Then I thought I heard something.

Listening, my ears heard some kind of deep, hoarse laughter.

I grabbed an oil lamp and headed towards the portrait room. I was scared but wanted to find Constance. I wanted to find her and get the hell out of this cursed place.

As I got closer, I could hear voices and faint, yet eerie music.

I stopped at the door, not wanting to proceed but knowing I had no choice.

Quickly, I opened the door. Much to my surprise, the portrait was back on the wall. Peter's body was still on the floor.

There, being pulled into the portrait by some dark entity, was Constance. I knew she had been seduced by the evil from within it. I screamed and threw the oil lamp at the *Sufletul Mortii,* now fully understanding its meaning.

Fire broke out when the lamp crashed and exploded on the wall, erupting the room in flames.

I ran out of there as the fire began to spread throughout the old monastery. I could hear screams and moans, intermingled with the hoarse laughter coming from the portrait.

I made my way out of the monastery into the rain, and down the road running in to the blackened evening. I found my way to a nearby town where I collapsed and was taken to the hospital.

For all anyone knew, my companions and I sought refuge overnight at the old monastery when an oil lamp fell over; causing the fire that killed my friends. When I recovered, I went home, where I kept my secret.

That was over twenty years ago.

I had hoped the oil lamp destroyed the *Sufletul Mortii*

and for years believed that it had.

Then one day I noticed an auction at Christie's dealing with an art auction of rarely seen portraits and paintings and felt compelled to attend.

I saw Constance—her Doppelganger, albeit older—reminding me that the real Constance had been pulled into the portrait. Her double was affixing a portrait to an easel for display.

A chill went up my spine.

It was the first time I saw the portrait in over twenty years.

I was sure the portrait knew I was there. I was disturbed to discover that an anonymous benefactor spent millions purchasing the *Sufletul Mortii* for a record price. Its wicked beauty was beheld by many that day, and it ensnared a new victim.

The portrait was back, and it brought with it all of the evil that had been hidden from the world for so long.

And I knew it was going to make up for lost time.

Smooth Sailing

Ezra Thompkins was perplexed.

Perplexed and more than a little concerned. As a sailor on board the schooner Excelsior he wondered about their destination and to where it was they were exactly heading.

It seemed like they were continuously sailing but never getting anywhere.

To him it appeared they had sailed for a great distance without seeing any land or shoreline, or any other ships.

He could not recall the last time they'd seen a port or when they had even left one. They were a ship's crew that were perpetually sailing from hither and yon.

Thompkins' frustration continued to grow and fester within as the rest of the crew continued doing their jobs. He could not believe the others were not even thinking or mentioning the same thing.

This sense of frustration was also beginning to personally alienate him from the rest of the crew. He was beginning to feel a sense of isolation as well. A congenial man in most regards, with average, indistinguishable looks, Thompkins was starting to show signs of this growing frustration while working with the other crew.

"Is something wrong?" his closest friend on the ship, Ned Glasgow, asked, noticing Thompkins' look of concern.

"Yeah," Thompkins responded, with a glum, defeated tone in his voice.

"What is it, Ezra?" Glasgow asked. "You alright?"

"I don't know, Ned, maybe it's just me," Thompkins

replied. "Maybe it's just me."

"What's troubling you buddy?" Glasgow asked again.

Thompkins looked at Glasgow handily and then replied. "You know, Ned, I've been thinking," he stated.

"Uh, oh," Glasgow said, interrupting him. "Thinking will only get you in trouble."

"No, Ned, listen," Thompkins continued, his frustration starting to grow. "You're missing my point. We should have seen a ship, a shore or even a damned seagull since we've been here. We haven't seen anything."

Glasgow looked at Thompkins quizzically. "What do you mean?" he asked.

"Ned, when was the last time you've seen a seagull?" Thompkins asked. "I know I haven't, and I can't even recall the last time I did see one."

"I think that's great, myself," Glasgow responded. "They're terrible."

"How about a ship then?" Thompkins asked.

"You worry too much," Glasgow responded. "You think too much. We'll get there. You'll see. The captain will get us where we're going."

"Ned, where are we going?" Thompkins asked. "Do you know exactly? Because I sure don't."

Glasgow was starting to get frustrated himself. "No, I don't," he muttered, rubbing his chin. "But the captain does and that's good enough for me. Trust me Ezra, the captain knows what he's doing."

Thompkins just took a deep breath and exhaled. He was exasperated about everything. "I'm not worried, Ned!" he finally stated. "I'm just wondering. Just thinking, that's all."

"Well, quit," Glasgow ordered. "You'll drive yourself insane that way. Come on, we've got to swab the deck."

"Okay," Thompkins groaned, not looking forward to the duty. It seemed that they were always swabbing the deck and it was always clean even before they did so.

As the men worked, Thompkins looked over at the other crewmen doing their jobs as well. It was all so routing and mundane, day in and day out. They did the same jobs every day.

Thompkins could not help but wonder if the rest of the crew felt and thought the same way as Glasgow. He hoped not, but greatly suspected they all did. Especially since he appeared to be the only one bringing it up at this point.

When he and Glasgow finished, Thompkins went below and crashed on his bunk. He was now tired on top of being frustrated.

As he laid there, he tried to remember leaving port. The more he thought about it, the more he could not even recall leaving home.

"Where was home?" he thought. *"Do I even have a home? How did I even get here? God, why don't I even remember? Am I going insane? God help me, what is going on?"*

After lying down for a couple of hours, he went back on deck to help his fellow crewmen. Once on deck he noticed they were still doing the same jobs as they were earlier.

"I've seen this before," he thought.

Thompkins then realized they had done the same exact thing every day with no change whatsoever. That was what bothered him as well. Their routine never changed. It stayed exactly the same without any deviation whatsoever, even in the smallest detail.

Once again, just like he always did, Thompkins helped with the ship's duties. That's what was expected of him and the others. Even if he had done it before, Thompkins repeated it. That was life on a ship.

That evening when he was lying in his bunk, he continued to wonder about his observations. The more he thought about it, the more questions he had. For the life of him, he could not remember his family, what they looked like or if he even had a family. Once exhaustion had overtaken him, he no longer thought or dreamed.

The next morning, he woke up and joined the crew back on deck. He could not help but notice that it was exactly the same as the day before. Everything and every little detail the same. Glasgow told him that they had swabbed the deck. Thompkins stood for a moment, watching his friend do so. He knew that they'd did this yesterday and the day before that.

Thompkins just watched. He felt like something just wasn't right and was totally askew.

"You alright?" First Mate Owen Dickerson asked, upon seeing Thompkins watch the others curiously, almost studying them.

Dickinson, while a bit taller, was close to Thompkins' age and had similar features to him and actually others on the Excelsior. Up until then, Thompkins had not realized just how similar they really were.

"I think so, Sir," Thompkins replied, looking at Dickinson. "I just….I just don't know about some things, that's all."

"Yes, yes," Dickerson stated. "Mr. Glasgow informed me that you had some misgivings."

"I wouldn't call them misgivings, Sir," Thompkins countered. "I would say they were more like questions to some observations I've been making."

Dickenson nodded, trying to assess what Thompkins had just said. "Right," he finally muttered. "I will bring it to the Captain Forbes' attention. Maybe he can address your concerns then. Will that do?"

Thompkins quietly nodded. "Okay," he sighed.

"Good," Dickerson replied. "Now go and assist Mr. Jones and Mr. Davis with their assignments."

"Yes, Sir," Thompkins responded before heading to work on the ship's rigging with the two crewmen. As he joined the two men, he was filled with a sense of Déjà vu'.

Once they finished, Thompkins walked quietly around the ship with only his thoughts. He could not shake the questions he had. They were weighing him down like an anchor to a ship. The difference being, Thompkins' thoughts navigated him with the buoyancy and seaworthiness of a rudderless ship.

Lost, troubled and uncertain.

Once again as he laid in his bunk at night, he was troubled by the same thoughts that he had the previous night. Even his observations were the same ones over and over again. Finally, like the night before, he fell asleep.

After once again swabbing the deck with his friend Glasgow, he relaxed by walking around the ship's deck, thinking. He'd grown restless and felt distanced from the other crewmembers.

After an hour of endless pacing and troubled wandering around the ship, the first mate finally returned to talk to him.

"The captain will see you now," Dickinson announced, placing his hand on Thompkins' shoulder. "He's at the helm. He'd like to hear your questions and concerns."

Thompkins nodded, then uttered hoarsely, "Yes, Sir."

"Let's go," Dickinson said, as he then escorted Thompkins to the captain.

Dickinson and Thompkins made their way to the captain, who was standing on the ship's bridge next to crewman Albert Hemmerlee, who was at the ship's wheel.

Captain Charles Forbes was an older man with white hair and a white beard and had a large pipe in his mouth. His pipe was *always* in his mouth. In spite of this, he had a grandfatherly, friendly look with a nice smile and clear blue eyes.

"Thompkins!" Captain Forbes exclaimed. "Mr. Dickinson informs me that you have some pretty serious concerns and maybe I can help to alleviate them."

Thompkins nodded. "I sincerely hope so, Sir," he replied.

"Well, Mr. Thompkins, tell me of your concerns," the captain stated.

Thompkins took a deep breath, then exhaled. "Well, Sir," he began hesitantly. "I was wondering several things. I have several questions."

"Alright," Captain Forbes replied. "Please continue."

"Well, Sir," Thompkins once again continued, "I've been making some observations and thinking about them. First off, we have been sailing for what seems like an eternity and haven't reached a destination. We haven't seen a shoreline, a port, another ship, a seagull or even a large wave on our voyage. Also, day in and day out, we do the same things over and over again, the exact same way. Every day is the same. There are no changes."

"Well, naturally Thompkins," Captain Forbes responded, before he and Dickinson chuckled, "You're on a ship, so there's bound to be some redundancy."

"No, Sir, it's not like that," Thompkins politely protested. "It's the same people doing the exact same things day in and day out. It never changes."

"That's because of the duty roster," Dickinson explained.

"Well, Sir, let's say it's exactly that," Thompkins continued. "How does that explain the lack of our seeing any ships or shoreline or even seagulls? Also, where are we sailing from and where are we sailing to?

Captain Forbes held his pipe in his teeth tightly, nodding. "Not to worry, laddy," he finally said with a warm and comforting smile. "Where we've been is unimportant. It's our destination that matters and we'll get there, I assure you."

"What about not seeing any other ships or shoreline?" Thompkins asked. "Don't you find that the least bit strange?"

Captain Forbes once again smiled. "Not one bit, Mr, Thompkins," he replied. "There have been times that I'd not seen a ship or a shoreline for what seemed like an eternity. Ease your worries laddy, we'll get to where we're going eventually. So, relax. Everything will be alright."

"Yes, Sir," Thompkins replied, softly. "I'll try. Thank you, Sir."

"That's good," Captain Forbes said. "I believe you are due to relieve Mr. Hemmerlee at suppertime while the crew eats. "Why don't you get some food and rest until then?"

"I'm not very hungry, Sir," Thompkins responded. "But, rest I can use."

"Very well then," Captain Forbes said. "Get some rest then."

"Yes, Sir," Thompkins said, saluting the captain before making his way below deck, still not really satisfied with the captain's explanation.

"He had a lot of questions," Dickinson commented as Thompkins walked away.

"That he did," Captain Forbes agreed. "That he did. Well, let's get back to our assignments, shall we?"

Once again, Thompkins went over his observations and questions he had in his head. Now he had even more. The weather was always clear, and the temperature was consistently the same. He began to realize that he never really noticed any clouds. Thompkins also noted that he never heard any of the crew talk about their homes, families, or where they were even from.

It was deeply troubling to him.

The captain only partially sated his desire for information.

Thompkins decided that maybe Glasgow was right. Maybe he *did* think too much. Maybe Glasgow was right in saying he would drive himself insane by thinking too much.

He had to relax and try his best to block out these troubling thoughts.

Finally, after a few minutes, exhaustion overtook him, and he fell asleep. Thompkins slept deeply and hard. He slept the sleep of troubled man who was mentally worn out from his own deep thoughts.

A few hours later, Thompkins relieved Hemmerlee at the helm so he could join the rest of the crew for supper. He also had to keep watch while the others were below. He knew that the rest of the crew thought he was making too much of his observations while being on the Excelsior.

Thompkins stood quietly, holding the wheel and keeping watch. He could not believe how quiet it was on the deck of the ship. There was no breeze or any sounds of the waves crashing against the hull of ship. There was complete silence.

He did his best to not think about all the questions that he'd been having.

Maybe Captain Forbes was right, he thought. Maybe his concerns and questions were easily answered, even if he couldn't think of what they were.

"*Sure, that was it,*" he thought.

After quite some time at the helm, Thompkins heard some laughter. Loud laughter. It sounded like it was all around him, but he could not see where it was coming from. Then he heard it coming from directly above where the ship was.

Thompkins looked up. He then saw a large cherubic

face looking down at him, smiling.

"Oh, my God!" he exclaimed in abject horror. "Captain! Captain! Mr. Dickinson! Mr. Dickinson! Ned!"

Thompkins called out to much of the crew but to no avail, to warn them of the *giant* that was looking down upon the ship. He then screamed and moved away from the wheel. The face appeared to be getting closer. He then began to backpedal as quickly as possible, screaming the entire time. Recoiling in terror, Thompkins eventually lost track of where he was, crashed backwards into the ship's rail, losing his balance, and fell overboard screaming.

Instead of splashing into water there was dull, ringing thud of hitting something hard.

Suddenly a voice from above called out, "Timmy! Get down from there!"

The little blond-haired boy moved away from the ship in the bottle that was setting in the large picture window of the study.

"Okay, Mama!" the little boy replied.

The mother came over to look at the ship in the bottle. "Your grandfather doesn't want you touching his ship in the bottle," she explained. "It's not a toy. Oh, look…one of the little crewmen has fallen off the ship. We'll have to tell him later that he needs to put him back."

"Okay, Mama," the little boy said again.

***

Lying on the glass that the schooner Excelsior sat in, Thompkins now stiff as a board finally had an answer to all of the questions and concerns he once had. He laid there like a piece of driftwood. A mere afterthought to those on board as well to the outside world. He now knew the Excelsior would continue its voyage to nowhere in a glass bottle on the study's window ledge by the port for its duration.

Man's Best Friend

It was all Thomas Collins could do to keep his composure. Try as he might to fight it, tears welled up in his eyes. Not one to cry easily, except when there was great joy or sadness, Collins could no longer keep his emotions in check.

He had always dreaded this day. No matter how hard he tried not to think about it, it finally came. He knew it would one day but did not want to deal with it then.

Now he had to, and it was tough.

Tough and emotionally heartbreaking.

Collins watched helplessly as his longtime loyal friend and family member was slowly dying. Father Time and old age had finally taken their toll.

He gently patted her head and stroked her back. She was comforted by his gentle, loving touch like many times before throughout the years. He loved her and she loved him back.

Collins broke down as she licked his hand in love and appreciation.

He always appreciated her affection, but now it was her saying goodbye. It was like she knew it was time to say farewell and that it would be alright. He knew that she loved them as much as they loved her. Somehow, he could tell that she was ready.

Having to put down their beagle Molly after well over fifteen years was personally devastating. It was one of the hardest things they ever had to do. Collins looked over at his wife, Colleen, who was bawling her eyes out. She had remained strong until Molly licked or kissed her goodbye as well and then she broke down.

Molly had really slowed down the last couple of years and began ailing for the last couple of months. She slowed down so much that even the occasional squirrel doing a tightrope walk across the power lines or the small chipmunk scurrying under the fence didn't make her give chase or even howl at them. She even had to be helped up and down from their bed and chairs at times.

After taking her to the veterinarian and seeing the growing and worsening health problem for Molly, they decided it was time. They could not bear to see her suffer like she was. It was an extremely tough and heartbreaking decision. She had held out so long because of the bond of love.

Unfortunately, it had to be done.

They watched as the veterinarian took Molly in back to shave her paw and give her a shot to relax her. When she returned, Molly was barely conscious, her breathing soft and unnoticeable.

Collins thought back on how, when they met Molly for the first time, that it had been love at first sight. He and his wife went to the dog pound to find a dog to adopt for their family. When an attendant had to clean her cage, he let her out to move her to another cage. Colleen crouched down to pet her, and Molly placed her frightened little head on Colleen's blue-jean-covered leg.

This ended their search rather quickly.

"I think we've been adopted," Collins observed.

"I think we've got a dog," Colleen agreed.

"She's a real good girl," the attendant said. "I was hoping someone would take her home soon. She's been here a while."

"She's got a home now," Collins replied.

"She sure does," Colleen agreed. "Let's go, Tom."

And they truly had. She had adopted the Collins'.

Love at first sight had won out.

For well over fifteen years their kids grew up and went off to college, and Molly had been a fixture in the family. Whether it was celebrating birthdays and holidays, going on vacations or other trips, Molly had taken part in all of it like any other family member.

They loved her and she loved them. She was more than a pet, she was family.

After the kids returned home from college or after being away for some time, she whimpered and cried, excited to see them like they were her own. The family in turn bought her treats and toys for her at Christmas and the day they adopted her was now her official birthday.

Even just sitting around the firepit in their backyard, Molly stayed close to them. They were her family and she loved and protected them as much as a little beagle could.

Now it was sadly time to say goodbye.

As Molly received the last injection, her life was now slipping away. She just seemed to drift off for an eternal sleep. It had been that easy. Her body finally had just shut down. After checking her for a pulse, the veterinarian nodded, saying she was gone.

The Collins both broke down and cried while petting their little four-legged girl and holding each other and saying how much they loved her.

"She was a good girl," Tom sobbed.

Colleen just nodded in agreement finally muttering a hoarse, "Yes."

Home would not be the same without her. She had been a fixture for such a long time it would be strange to not have her around any longer.

Afterwards they took Molly home, burying her in what was her favorite spot in the back yard. It was a nice sunny spot that was not far from the back fence, where an overhanging mulberry tree was and where she could keep a vantage point to see any squirrel. or chipmunks.

She had spent many times either lying in the sun there or patrolling the yard, standing guard against those chattering, annoying and invading terrorist squirrels and chipmunks.

Now even the squirrels would be missing the Molly's due diligence as protector of the family yard and realm, for the terror of all squirrel and chipmunk-dom was now gone. Gone to pass over that rainbow bridge where all four-legged family members go to wait for their family members and loved ones.

For the first week after Molly was gone, neither Tom or Colleen had the heart to move her toys and old bed that she laid on for the most part. It was too painful. It was also strange not sharing a bed, a couch or a chair with her anymore. He had always been at their sides.

Finally, after a couple of months, they put her bed and toys in a closet for safekeeping.

The only reminder they had of her were pictures of her looking happy with family members and by herself on their refrigerator.

"Do you think we should get another dog?" Colleen asked at dinner one night.

"No, not yet," Tom replied. "I think we both need more time to grieve. I know I do. We will eventually, just not right now."

"Okay," Colleen agreed.

When their youngest, their daughter Elizabeth, returned home to visit from her place in Minnesota that weekend, she found their home kind of sad and empty.

"Wow!" Elizabeth said, carrying in some of her travel bags in through the door. "I was half expecting Molly to come running to see me."

"Yeah," Tom admitted. "We felt that way for about a week. It was strange. She would see us off in the morning and greet us when we returned home. I still miss her."

"Me too," Elizabeth agreed. "She whimpered and cried every time I came back from school because she missed me."

Tom and Colleen just quietly nodded in agreement.

When their other children Jon and Kathleen showed up for their little family reunion they were also struck by how quiet and different the house was, now that Molly was gone.

After dinner they sat around and reminisced about their four-legged family member.

"Remember she'd trampled Mom's flower garden trying to chase those damned squirrels when they were on the power lines?" Jon asked, while laughing. "Mom would get so mad then a half an hour later she'd be giving her a treat."

Colleen gave an anguished look. "Oh, I would not," she protested.

"Yeah, you would, Mom," Kathleen disagreed.

"They're right honey," Tom agreed.

"Oh, maybe one time," Colleen argued.

Everybody exchanged looks, knowing that wasn't the case.

"Mom, it was more than that," Elizabeth finally stated. "We've all seen you do it more than once."

"Alright, alright, maybe it was a couple of times," Colleen finally admitted.

"Yeah, okay," Tom commented, not believing her.

"Say, Dad, did you say she was owned by an older couple or something?" Jon asked.

"Yeah," Tom replied. "I guess she was owned by an older couple. From what we were told the old man died about a year or so after buying her for his wife as a puppy. After that his wife became sick and bedridden and could not properly care for her. When she died, her family dropped her off to the pound. We were able to get her a short time later. She was very friendly and well-behaved."

"She was a loving dog," Kathleen stated. "It seemed like when anyone one of us was sick she stayed with us. It was like she was making sure we were alright or at least checking on us."

"That's right," Elizabeth agreed. "Even when we had colds, there she was snuggling with us."

"Well, there is a reason for that," Tom started to explain. "You see she wasn't your dog. You were her kids. She felt you were hers."

"That's right," Jon agreed. "She was very protective of us. Even if she wasn't that big."

"Yeah, she never did like that one guy named Andrew that I went to school with," Kathleen said. "She must have been able to see what he actually was as a person. Who would have thought he would have got put in prison for robbing houses?"

"Yeah, he was a real winner," Colleen laughed.

"That's true," Elizabeth agreed. "But all one had to do was say hello and say her name and she was their friend. She loved everybody."

"Except strangers and people walking by she didn't recognize," Colleen countered. "She'd howl like no tomorrow. One time she let me know to call the police when someone was trying to see inside the window. I think they were casing the place. She might have been a little dog, but she knew how to protect us the best way that she could."

"Whatever became of that?" Jon asked.

"The police nabbed them," Colleen responded. "I guess they were part of burglary ring. Associates of Andrew's I guess."

"Molly was a hero," Kathleen said.

"Yeah," Tom agreed. "She was a good girl alright.

Well, let's go out to the fire pit and relax. It's too nice to be in here."

They went outside. Immediately the kids noticed the dug-up spot where Tom and Colleen and had buried Molly. Tom through some kindling and wood in the firepit pour on some gasoline and lit the fire for them to sit around.

"So, that's the spot," Jon observed.

"Yeah," Tom admitted. "I was thinking of getting her a little headstone or something. I don't know. Maybe plant some flowers there."

"Awww, that's so sweet," Elizabeth said. "I think that is so nice. I'll help pay for one."

"So, will I," Kathleen announced.

"Yeah, me too," Jon agreed.

"We'll make it real nice," Colleen stated. "She deserved it."

The rest of the evening the family sat around making small talk about school, jobs, careers, work, friends, and life in general as they watched the flames flicker into the night.

"Dad, do you believe that thing about their being a rainbow bridge for our pets when they die?" Jon asked out of the blue.

Tom thought for a moment then nodded. "Yeah, I think I do," he admitted. "I have to believe there is. I truly hope there is too, because I would like to see all of the animals that I have loved in my life again. Why do you ask?"

"Because, someone I know says animals don't have any souls so they don't get into Heaven," Jon explained.

"Sounds like a religious zealot," Colleen snapped. "That, or they never had a pet in their life."

"Look, I think any animal that loves you or in this case returns your love and affection, has a place there,"

Tom said. "How can anyone say they don't have souls when that animal has a personality and love you too? To me it goes beyond reason."

"Amen," Kathleen agreed.

"Yeah," Elizabeth added.

"Anything that can love you back has to have a soul," Tom continued. "They have to have something. Some kind of soul or whatever you want to call it. Besides, I think heaven would be pretty boring and sad without animals."

"Yeah, it would," Colleen agreed.

"I would never say that Molly didn't have a soul," Tom added.

"Me neither," Colleen agreed. "That's the problem with some of these overly religious types, they get lost in the doctrine and don't think sometimes."

"That's kinda what I think too," Jon admitted.

"I think it also sells the animal short too," Tom stated. "Like I said, if they have the capacity to learn, love and protect, then they must have a soul."

"I won't say that's deep, dad, but it does make a lot of sense," Elizabeth said.

"Thanks," Tom replied.

"Oh, that reminds me," Colleen remembered. "Speaking of deep, I called my cousin about coming over and checking out the furnace. It's been sounding funny and running a little rough lately."

"Oh, okay," Tom replied. "That's good. Because I sure wouldn't know how to work on it. Then again, I'm not a heating and cooling guy either."

"Good thing," Colleen joked.

"Yeah, well I admit my shortcomings," Tom responded. "I can do carpentry, roofing and some basic repairs. Anything beyond the basics of electricity, plumbing, heating and cooling and I'm lost. I'll admit that.

I know my limitations."

"Well, I'm heading it," Jon announced. "The mosquitoes are starting to make a meal out of me."

"Yeah, me too," Kathleen admitted.

"Let's head in then," Colleen said.

"Yeah, the fire's about burned itself out anyway," Tom agreed.

They all headed inside for the remainder of the evening where they kept talking. Eventually Colleen pulled out some ice cream for them to have as late dessert. A few hours later they turned in for the night.

As they slept, the furnace that Tom and Colleen knew needed some work began to act up. It made an unusual noise that grew a little louder and ran a little rougher. The heat exchanger covered with soot and dirt began to emit carbon monoxide and smoke.

The carbon monoxide being a colorless and odorless gas was not detectable. The soot covered heat exchanger cause the smoke to billow out of the furnace vents in the living and dining rooms and others closest to the furnace, filling the air with its toxins.

After having made it over the rainbow bridge where she felt no pains from old age, no longer felt ill and was once again young and energetic, Molly, the Collins' beloved beagle, could sense that her family was in danger.

Grave danger.

While she might not have known exactly what kind it was and what it could do, Molly knew their lives were in jeopardy.

Instinctively, Molly knew what she had to do. She had to save her family. She had to cross back over that rainbow bridge and save the family that she loved for most of her life.

She loved them too much not to. They were after all 'her people' and her family. Even from here, she knew it was her duty to protect them anyway that she could for one last time. They had been too good to her and she knew how much they loved her.

Her love and loyalty knew no bounds. For they were her family and always would be.

Forever and ever.

So, Molly crossed that rainbow bridge on her mission to protect her family as best as she knew how. Once back she did the only thing that would alert the family. Molly began to howl as loudly as she could. It was all she could do.

Sometime in the middle of the night, Tom thought he heard the distinct howling of a dog. Not just any dog, but their dog.

Their Molly.

But, how could that be? She was gone. At first Tom thought it was a dream, but it grew louder and more distinct. He could no longer ignore it.

"Molly?" he asked, only partially awake.

"What is that?" Colleen asked, coming out of a sound sleep. "Molly?"

Soon both of them climbed out of bed. Tom sensed something wasn't right and he went out to check as they continued to hear their long-loved and departed dog continue to howl some kind of warning or alert. Soon the kids were also up and in the hallway as well

"What's going on?" Jon asked.

"Was that Molly?' Elizabeth asked. "It, sure sounds like her."

Tom headed out towards the living room ad was greeted by billowing smoke from coming from the vents. He was soon joined by the rest of the family.

"Is there a fire?" Kathleen asked.

"No, it's the furnace acting up," Tom replied. "Everybody open the windows. I'll shut it off. Then get out of here. There's carbon monoxide coming out, so get outside once were done."

Everybody started opening all of the windows. After a few minutes they had them all open.

As Tom closed the door to the furnace room, he turned around and saw Molly standing near the back door. She wagged her tail, then turned and literally passed through the door. He stared in shock and disbelief. He then regained his composure and yelled for everybody to head out the door to the back patio.

"Everybody alright?" Tom asked.

He was greeted with a chorus of "Yeahs."

"What happened?" Kathleen asked. "Did the furnace start a fire?"

"No," Tom replied. "It just broke down that's all. It was probably just the heat exchanger. It was probably covered by soot. That's why all of the smoke."

"Wow," Colleen gasped.

"Yeah, when these things go bad, they emit carbon monoxide," Tom explained. "It could have killed us."

"My God," Elizabeth gasped. "It was Molly. Molly woke us all up. It was her barking. She woke us up and saved us."

"Are we sure?" Jon asked. "I heard a dog, but we can't be sure it was her."

"It was," Colleen stated. "I'd know her howl anywhere."

For some reason Tom decided to turn around and look at Molly's gravesite. He had an uncanny feeling he should look over there. The rest of his family followed suit and looked over there as well.

Standing in front of the spot that was her final resting place, stood their beagle Molly. Her mouth was open and panting as if she were smiling and happy.

"Oh, my God," Colleen gasped, tears running down

her eyes.

The Collins stood in stark silence and shock upon seeing her.

Molly then turned around, her tail wagging. She looked back one last time and entered a kind of white portal with a kind mutli-colored walkway or rainbow type bridge inside it. She then went on her way back to where she had come from.

Tears welled up in all their faces.

"Wow," Jon muttered. "She really did save our lives."

Kathleen and Elizabeth started crying. Colleen still crying moved over and hugged them, trying to comfort them.

For now, they truly knew that the little dog that they had loved, loved them so much that it returned to save them. They also knew that she was alright and in a better place. As the Collins stood outside, they realized there was a special kind of magic in the love they shared as a family with Molly.

That love itself was the greatest magic.

The Ghost of Tom

Have you seen the ghost of Tom?
Long white bones with the rest all gone
Have you seen the ghost of Tom?
Ooo-oo-oo-oo-oo-oo-ooh
Long white bones with the rest all gone
Wouldn't it be chilly with no skin on? Ooo-oo-oo-oo-oo-oo-ooh
-Children's song

This story is really hard to believe, even for us right now. We still talk about it from time to time. I am not saying that I or even the rest of us believe in ghosts, or anything like that, but after this incident, I'm not so sure we'll be so quick to dismiss any tales either.

It is all pretty unbelievable.

If it wasn't ghosts, then somebody is playing one hell of a trick on us.

In fact, they may be playing a joke on us as a form of payback.

Then again, who really knows?

It all started when our cousin Tom passed away. After getting what he called a pretty good buzz at a party and carrying on with his wife, he died in his sleep. He had been a good guy, even if he did occasionally do things in excess. He had been a party animal in his younger days. He always offered to help when we needed it, fun to be around, told a lot of bad jokes, played numerous practical jokes and pretty much spoke his mind, so you always knew where he stood on things. He lived a good and full life, not to mention a happy one.

It is still hard to believe he is gone…we were all pretty close. In fact, I shared the same first name. Our mothers had us about the same time, shared the same hospital room after delivery, so that was partly it. In a sense, we had always been a little closer than the others were.

Story goes, the lucky bastard died in his sleep after having sex with his wife. He always said that was the way he wanted to go. He said it sure beat getting hit by a Mack truck or dying of cancer. And he did have cancer once. He always joked he would have come and gone in the same night. And well, luckily for him, he did.

The day of the showing was nice. The type of summer day that he always enjoyed. A nice, sunny, warm day. Then again, he always said God shined on him throughout his whole life. Why should today be any different?

Like all funerals, the whole family turned out. That included his immediate family, wife, kids, grandkids, brother, in-laws, cousins, second, third, and fourth cousins, friends, old co-workers, acquaintances and others who knew and loved him. We had grandparents who had ten kids and they all averaged three kids each and we all averaged three and so on and so on.

Putting it bluntly, there was a hell of a crowd there. The funeral home had broken out all the extra chairs that it had on hand and it still wasn't enough. There was standing room only.

Wall to wall people.

Different groups of teary-eyed people offering their condolences to his wife and kids, laughing, shaking their heads and talking about Tom. Many were just reminiscing about him with the more memorable and funny stories. Believe me there were plenty. Like his streaking down

Dequindre Road and 13 Mile Road on the night of his bachelor party, driving through a McDonald's naked and asking for Big Macs with extra sauce, farting next to a local politician and blaming him for it, mooning a cop on New Year's Eve of 1979, getting drunk in a bar, pouring mustard on himself and yelling "I'm the goddamn mustard man" and so on. You get the idea, the man had fun. And, a lot of it. Sometimes too much. We were always surprised that he never needed to be bailed out of jail, especially when he was younger.

You could basically catch parts of sentences people were saying like "That crazy…" or "I can't believe it…" or "He was a good guy…" and "He always said what he thought…didn't stab anybody in the back…always helped out…he had a lot of fun in life…"

Sentiments we all shared about the man.

When somebody first approached the casket, they were greeted with a pretty unusual sight. He was dressed in his favorite blue jeans, an ugly blue Hawaiian shirt, tennis shoes, with a loosened Three Stooges tie. He seemed to have a bit of a grin or smirk on his face, like he had heard or knew of a joke and he was the only one in on it. Beside him was his Detroit Tiger baseball cap that he had gotten signed many years ago by Hall of Famer Al Kaline. He also had two sports cards of Kaline and Gordie Howe, his two favorite athletes of all-time. He also had an old t-shirt with Rod Serling on it draped in the casket.

"That sonofabitch…" my brother Jim exclaimed. "He's got that same expression he had when he let a bad fart near us, and nobody realized it was him."

"He died a happy man," Tom's brother Tim announced. "I hope I'm that lucky."

Jim went on to comment how he had some of his favorite items in the casket with him, which basically was old Detroit Tiger and Red Wing stuff. It was a tradition we did since our grandmother passed away back in 1986. Little things that we knew were part of what the person liked and was proud of, but nothing outrageously valuable.

"I see, the Tigers and Red Wings are represented," another cousin, Bob, commented as he walked up next to us. "I see he hasn't got any Lions stuff in there with him."

"Shit, you know he wouldn't be caught dead with Lions stuff in there," Tim laughed. "He hated the Lions. He enjoyed heckling them when they lost. They still haven't won a Super Bowl. He was right about them."

"Hell, I remember that game when he gave up on them," I said. "It was 1970 and the day after Christmas and most of us came back over Grandma's to help do something in the basement with the uncles. They finished working on it by game time and we sat and ate leftovers. A few of you weren't around. Anyways, Tommy bet Uncle Bunky that the Lions would win. He had just earned $45. Bill Munson came in and threw an interception late when they were driving on the Cowboys and they lost 5-0, on a field goal and a safety. There was a bonfire outside, and he took all of his Lions wear and even his football cards and hats and burned it all. He never cheered them on again. In fact, he hated the Lions ever since. If he watched them, it was to make fun of them and their ineptitude."

"That's right," Tim said. "He said that if they ever won anything it would be the end of the world, doomsday to be exact, or he'd be dead first. He sure loved to hate that team."

"Remember the time when they went winless and he yelled 'interception' before the quarterback threw an interception?" Bob asked. "Half the bar looked over at him, really pissed and he just laughed, 'I can't help it your team sucks.' God, I didn't think we'd get out of there alive but ended up having a great time even with the Lions fans there."

"That was a riot," Jim agreed.

"It sure was," Tim chuckled.

"We ought to put a Lions jersey or pennant in there with him, as a last joke," Jim suggested.

"I don't know, man." Tim muttered. "He'll probably haunt your ass. And I don't believe in that shit. But he would haunt your ass and he'd be the guy to do it."

"That would be great!" Bob exclaimed. "I owe him big time for the inflatable doll prank he pulled on me, twenty years ago. I never did pay him back for that."

"Yeah, and I owe him for sending that fat, ugly stripper to my 50th birthday. I swear to God, she looked like Grosie O'Connell. She was larger than I was."

Just then two more cousins, Bob and John, who were brothers, walked up. Jim filled them in on what he was thinking about doing. John passed, he had been a marine and just didn't like the idea of pulling jokes on the dear departed as he called it. He said it didn't seem right. Besides, he said Tom hadn't pulled any worse jokes on him than he pulled back. He didn't feel the time was right.

Bob was neither here nor there on it. He thought it would be great if Jim and our other cousin Bob did it, but he didn't want to really be involved.

"What about you?" Bob asked.

"I don't think so," I responded. "I was asked to speak on behalf of the cousins, so I better not."

"Do you have a Lions pennant or Jersey? Jim asked Bob.

"Nope,"

"There's a sporting goods store just down the road, I'll go in half with you on some Lions stuff, if you want to do it," Jim offered.

"Deal!" Bob exclaimed.

So, Jim and Bob discreetly left the funeral home to put their plans in motion, while the rest of us mingled and visited with each other and reminisced about Tom's life.

Within fifteen minutes they were back with some generic Lions jersey with a number twenty-four on it.

"You guys don't think it will bother the family, do you?" I asked.

Tim spoke up for the first time. "Hard to tell, just be careful when doing it," he cautioned. "I don't want his wife and kids upset."

"We will just shove it down under him or something," Jim explained. "Besides, we're all pallbearers and we're the only ones who know about it."

Jim took the jersey and placed it just under Tom's leg in the casket, without anybody hardly noticing. He stood there nonchalant still talking to Bob, Tim and myself. A few seconds later a real bad smell permeated the air near us. It was as if somebody had cracked a real, bad one off.

"Goddamn, Tim, did you have to shit your, pants?!" Bob said, with a look of disgust.

"Hey, I didn't," Tim responded. "I thought it was one of you."

We all looked at each other, figuring somebody wasn't telling the truth about which one of us farted.

"It was probably Tom," said Jim. "Cracking one off for old times' sake for us to remember him by. Man, next to some of the uncles he was one of the worse at passing gas."

I looked back at Tom and could have almost sworn that his grin was a little more like a smirk.

We then walked away and started talking to other friends and family members for the next few minutes about our cousin and how everybody was doing.

I really don't know who noticed it first, but I was talking to one of Tom's oldest and best friends, Mike, when I happened to look over and saw a female friend of Tom's picking up something off of the floor. It was the

Lions jersey.

I walked over and explained what it was and why it was there. She laughed and handed me the jersey.

"Hey, what's going on? Jim came back up and asked.

"Somebody found it on the floor," I replied.

"Somebody must have removed it," Jim surmised.

"I don't know," I said. "I didn't see anything or anybody."

Jim took the jersey and refolded it and put it back in the casket underneath the pillow underneath Tom's head. It was out of sight and mind.

"There," he announced. "It's in a different spot and nobody will be the wiser."

Just then Bob came up. "What are you doin'?" he asked.

"It was on the floor and I'm just putting it back," Jim answered.

"How did it get out in the first place?" Bob asked

"Beats the hell outta me," Jim replied.

Jim and Bob walked away, but continued to keep an eye on the casket to make sure they could see who really removed the Lions jersey.

I knew it wasn't me, because I was trying to figure out what I was going to say, and I wasn't much of a speaker. I also knew it wasn't Tim, because he was busy with family members and helping do things for Tom's family at the funeral.

Jim soon went out to have a cigarette and Bob had to take a leak. When they got back in, they found the Lions jersey back on the floor next to the casket. There was also that bad fart smell, nearby.

"Seriously," Jim said to me, about the jersey. "Are you messing with us?"

"No, Jim, I don't have time," I responded.

Bob looked skeptical about my reply but did not say

anything. "If you're not, then somebody is," he finally mumbled.

"Yeah, but, who?" Jim asked.

"I couldn't tell you," I responded. "I don't have a clue."

We continued to visit with family and friends. During that time, we all kept our eye on the casket to make sure that nobody was taking anything out. A few people put mementos in it, and kissed Tom's forehead, but that was it. They walked away without any clue as to there being a Lions jersey in the casket.

By nine p.m. the showing was winding down for the evening and people were slowly shuffling out. Jim went back to check on the Lions jersey to see if it was still there.

"What the fu…?" he said as he lifted up the pillow to see that the jersey was gone. "Where in the hell is it?"

Bob, Tim and I walked back over to the casket.

"Is it gone again?" Bob asked.

"It's probably Tom's ghost, throwing the jersey out," laughed Tim. "You know he hated the Lions."

Jim finally looked behind the casket and found the jersey between the casket and the wall on the floor.

"Here it is," Jim announced. "I will put it down near his feet this time and I will stay right here until just about everybody is gone."

Jim complained later that the fart odor he smelled earlier was back again as well.

We had all been to enough of these things to know that most of us never really left on time. It was as if everyone felt compelled to stay. By five after nine we were finally winding our way to the doors. Jim hung back near the casket to make sure nobody removed the jersey. Finally, the funeral home attendants came and closed up the casket, with the jersey still inside with Tom. The last of us left at twenty after nine, into a nice warm peaceful night.

Fitting, yet sad.

Tomorrow would be tough. We all knew it well. We had come to regard it as the big send-off or the big show. The actual funeral itself.

The next day came and like clockwork we were all there early. As soon as we were let into the parlor, the first thing we saw was that damned Detroit Lions jersey on the floor next to the casket.

"So, what are you going to do now?" Bob asked.

"I'm going to put the sucker back in there, just before it gets closed for the last time," Jim answered.

The funeral service was beautiful. It brought tears of both sadness and laughter to just about everybody's eyes. A few of us got up and told our stories and shared our memories of the deceased. It was one of the best, and sad to say, funniest funerals I had ever been to. Four of us as speakers and we all pretty much nailed the eulogy to a 'T.' We knew the family loved it.

Everyone paid their final respects with the immediate family being last.

Just afterwards, Jim placed the jersey back into the casket, down near Tom's feet, before the funeral home staff closed the casket. "It's now his jersey forever," he announced

Bob laughed. "Remind me not to tell you what I don't like."

"I think we're getting a little old for this shit, anyway," I commented.

So, we loaded the casket into the hearse, got in our vehicles and headed towards the cemetery in our long funeral procession. Once there, we carried the casket to the grave site and lowered it onto the straps that would lower it into its final resting place.

"Okay, everybody please take your places so we can

start the last of the service,' the funeral director said.

The minister told us to bow our heads in prayer and recited the Lord's prayer. The service was concluded, and we were on our way back to our vehicles that were parked nearby so we could head to the luncheon afterward. As we stood there talking for a moment, one of the funeral home people approached us.

"I found this on the ground next to the casket," the attendant said. "It's a Lions jersey. Somebody must have dropped it."

Jim's eyes were as big as saucers. His mouth was open, and he was in shock. I don't think I had ever seen him in his seventy-odd years this shocked.

I took the jersey. "Thanks," I said as the attendant left and I handed Jim the jersey. "You want to give it back again?"

"Yeah, do it, Jim" Bob interjected. "Throw it in on top."

Jim just nodded. The casket was being lowered and he threw the jersey in. He told the cemetery attendants it was alright, his cousin told him to do it. The problem was the cousin who told him wasn't Tom.

Tim walked over to us. "I told you he hated the Lions," he commented.

"Well, I didn't see anybody remove it," Bob said, trying to figure it out. "We were the only sonsofbitches who knew it was in there. I didn't see anything, and now I'm damn glad I didn't. This is unbelievable."

We all agreed.

We then left for the luncheon where we spent much of the day talking and fondly reminiscing about him. While a sad occasion, there was much fun and joy talking about his life.

None of us still know what to think or believe.

I just think back to what Tom said. "He wouldn't be

caught dead in a Lions jersey, or with any Lions stuff."

True to his word, he wasn't. The only time he wore one was when he lost a bet and that he was glad to do because he beloved Red Wings won.

One day later, I got a call from Jim who had to tell me that he and his wife went home, after staying at our place after the funeral. It turns out that once they got home, they found a dirt-covered Lions jersey hanging over their dining room chair. It still had the price tag, from where Jim and Bob had bought it before the funeral. Jim's wife was cussing him out for leaving his dirty outdoor work clothes on the chair and not in the hamper. He also said that there was a really bad smell, like a really bad fart in his house. They had to open the windows to clear it out.

Jim threw the jersey away and never played another joke on anybody ever again, including and especially any dead relatives.

I don't know if any of us believe in ghosts or not, but I know none of us are ruling anything out. I just know that when I watched another potential Lions quarterback throw another interception on what appeared to be a fluke, during their first pre-season game, I could not help but wonder if that was Tom heckling his least favorite football team from the great beyond.

Sometimes when we still get together, we try to rationalize what really happened. We wonder whether maybe somebody was playing a joke on all of us, or if it really was the ghost of Tom. Hard telling, but one thing's for sure: the Lions still suck and according to Tom, doomsday is still some time away because of that fact.

I think one day we will all find out.

Last Dance at the Stardust Ballroom

For Mildred Dunlap it was the start of another day at the Autumn Years Nursing Home. The octogenarian had been a resident there for just under a year after her husband Henry passed away. Afflicted with dementia and a slew of other health ailments that came with old age, she was pretty much confined to either her bed or her wheelchair for most of the day.

The few visitors she had included her sister Ruth, her children Henry, Roger and Lillian as well as the occasional visit from her grandchildren and a couple of friends that were still living and physically able to visit when time permitted.

Her days consisted of going to the bathroom, breakfast, getting dressed, with some assistance from the staff and pretty much watching an almost endless onslaught of daytime television that was usually interrupted by a daily and much-needed nap.

She really had no place to go and no ability to get there if she did. She was not only a prisoner of sorts to the nursing home but her own body as well.

At five-foot-two and with almost pure white hair, Mildred was a shell of her former younger self that was basically biding her time and waiting to die.

Mildred sat patiently as the housekeeping staff brought in her breakfast tray. It had the usual egg substitute, multi-grain toast, grayish-colored gruel-like oatmeal, prune juice, coffee and the usual utensils and prescribed seasonings that she found tolerable at best.

Mildred stared blankly at her culinary extravaganza with mixed feelings. Even in her condition, she was not a fan of this particular menu, but was hungry and needed to eat. After a few moments of hesitation, Mildred began to nibble at her meal. It wasn't great, but it would do for now.

A short time after breakfast, a medical staff member, a young nurse's assistant named Amy Howard, came in to check on her. Amy was friendly and a very bubbly personality that Mildred enjoyed seeing almost every day.

"Good morning!" Amy exclaimed upon entering the room. "How are you today?" Mildred just quietly smiled and nodded. Amy could somehow tell by her expression that the answer was 'good' in spite of not saying a word. "That's good."

She then helped Mildred to get dressed and then had an attendant help her into a wheelchair. Amy could tell that Mildred felt better about being dressed and moved.

"I think you're having a visitor today," Amy announced.

Mildred gave a look of acknowledgment to the young nurse's assistant.

"Yeah, it's your sister," Amy added. "She usually visits on this day. She should be by shortly."

Mildred knew that her sister Ruth made it a point to visit at least once a week. If there was a holiday or a special event like her birthday or some other occasion it was twice a week. She just wished that her own children visited as often. Usually they visited once every other week and that was for only an hour or so.

Because of Mildred's health issues and advancing dementia Ruth usually did all of the talking. Which she had done a lot of the talking even before Mildred was diagnosed with dementia. She had, as Mildred once observed, always been a "Chatty Kathy" since she was very young.

Ruth had been the baby of the family behind Mildred and her three older brothers Norman, Wesley and Stanley. Sadly, now there was only the two of them left.

While she was unable to really express it, Mildred really looked forward to and appreciated Ruth's visit. Ruth herself lost her own husband, Robert, only a few months before Mildred's husband Henry passed away.

Ruth arrived shortly after lunch time, and when Amy was once again checking on her. Ruth looked somewhat similar to Mildred, except that she was younger, less frail looking and a little taller. She was also carrying a larger bag with some kind of book or photo album in it.

"Hello Mildred, how are you doing today?" Ruth asked

Mildred nodded and smiled. She was glad to see Ruth, even if at times she had trouble remembering who she was.

"She's doing well today," Amy answered. "She seems in good spirits."

"Well, that's good," Ruth said, reaching out and touching her sister's hand, then leaning over to kiss her cheek.

"She always looks forward to your visits," Amy added.

"How is she doing?" Ruth asked, as she sat down in a chair next to Mildred.

"About the same," Amy replied with almost an exasperated sigh. "She doesn't talk much anymore. I think she no longer can because of her dementia. But you will have to talk to the doctors more about that. Other than she has been gradually getting less responsive verbally. That's just my take, but I am just a nurse's assistant."

Ruth sighed and shook her head, then stroked the back of Mildred's thinning, white hair. "That's sad," she finally muttered. "You wouldn't know it now, but she was young and vibrant once. She loved to dance. Mildred and her husband Henry would go to the Stardust Ballroom almost every Saturday night and dance the night away."

"The Stardust Ballroom?" Amy asked. "Was that like a club or something?"

"Yeah, it was an old dance hall," Ruth explained. "They played jazz, swing and all kinds of music. We heard everything from Tony Bennett to Miles Davis to Stan Kenton, Jimmy Dorsey, and Louis Armstrong. It was a real swinging place."

"Oh, how sweet," Amy cooed. "I'll bet she was absolutely stunning and the belle of the ball so to speak."

Ruth looked over at her sister and smiled. "That she was," she said. "She absolutely was. Her and Henry sure could cut a rug."

"Wow," Amy replied. "That's great! I bet they made a handsome couple."

"In fact, I brought and old photo album," Ruth announced. "It's in my bag. Her wedding anniversary is coming up. Isn't it dear?"

Both Amy and Ruth looked over at Mildred and saw her smiling and nodding her head. Somehow, miraculously, of all the memories that her dementia and failing health had stolen from her, she still had that one. She still remembered her anniversary and dancing at the Stardust Ballroom.

"She knows," Ruth finally commented. "I believe in my heart that she truly knows and remembers that."

Amy nodded in agreement. "So, when is her anniversary?" she asked.

"This Saturday," Ruth replied.

"Wow!" Amy responded. "How many years would

they have been married?"

"Sixty-five," Ruth answered, as she opened the photo album and shared it with Mildred who smiled and started looking at the old photos.

"Oh, can I see?" Amy asked, as she moved over to look at the photo album that was opened and spread across to two ladies' laps.

"Here is Mildred and Henry on the night they became engaged," Ruth explained.

Amy looked down at the old black and white photo. "They definitely made a real good-looking couple," she observed. "She was a real looker and her husband was pretty handsome as well."

"Yes, they were," Ruth agreed.

"Well, I have to go tend to my other duties," Amy announced. "I'll be back later. It was really nice talking to you."

"Thank you," Ruth replied. "The feeling is mutual."

As Amy left the room, Ruth started going through the photo album with Mildred.

Ruth pointed to a picture with multiple people in it. "There we are," she announced. "There's me and Robert, you and Henry, Sam and Denise Nichols, Bill and Carol Brundage and John and Mary Kendricks."

Ruth looked over at Mildred and could see her eye almost light up with delight and excitement. She could tell that Mildred had a look of some familiarity on her face.

"And here we all are at the beach," Ruth continued. "There's Stanley with his wife, Marion, Norman and his wife Ann and Wesley and Diane, along with us and our spouses. It was for a long weekend. We had a great time."

Ruth looked back over at Mildred, who was just observing. She wasn't sure Mildred remembered this but kept up the hope and belief that she did.

"Here we are at the Stardust Ballroom celebrating

your first anniversary," Ruth said, pointing at the pictures. "Boy, you two were a good-looking couple. I think everybody we knew was there that night. What a party. You two were so much in love. I think we all were back then. I think you ended up getting pregnant with Henry Jr. that night. It sure was a magic night."

Ruth smiled. She then noticed that Mildred had a similar smiled and light in her eyes over that photograph. She knew for sure that Mildred was able to recollect some of the memories attached to those photos. Especially the ones connected to the Stardust Ballroom.

They both spent the next few hours going through entire photo album.

Ruth then looked at her watch. "Oh my, look at the time," she announced. "It's getting late. I have to be going Millie. I'll be back Saturday, Mill, I love you. Oh, keep the album and look through all you want."

Ruth hugged her sister and left the room.

Once Ruth left, Mildred looked at the album and began to cry. Mildred knew that she missed the very things that they had looked at for the last couple of hours.

On her way out, Ruth stopped by the desk to talk to the medical staff.

"Hi, I am Mildred Dunlap's sister," Ruth announced. "Is there a doctor that I can talk to about my sister's condition?"

"Yes," the nurse at the desk replied as she turned around to talk to man seated partially behind her and off to the side that was looking at a patient's records. "Doctor Wilson, Mrs. Dunlap's sister has some questions for you."

"Oh, okay," Dr. Wilson said looking up. "How can I help you?"

Ruth looked at Dr. Wilson. He was a tall, handsome man in his early forties. He came out from behind the desk and shook Ruth's hand.

Ruth shook his hand. "I am Ruth Morgan, Mildred's sister," she said. "I was just curious how my sister is doing."

"Oh, yes," Dr. Wilson stated. "Oh, I am Dr. Jim Wilson. Anyway, she is stable for right now. However, I fear that she is only going to get worse. Her communications have deteriorated to the point where she doesn't talk at all. She has very little verbal communication."

"How's her memory?" Ruth asked. "I mean, I believe she recognized a couple of photos in my photo album that I left her but I'm not sure about the rest, though."

"Yeah," Dr. Wilson replied. "It's good that she is able to remember a few places and things. At least for now. But I am afraid that too will eventually go."

Ruth nodded. "I see," she groaned.

"It's good that you're coming and sharing photos with her," Dr. Wilson stated. "That just may help her to keep them a little longer. I know it cannot hurt. I think she might also need to see her own children more often as well. That can only help. It might buy her some kind of time."

Ruth nodded. "Thank you, Doctor," she said. "I truly appreciate it."

"Anytime," Dr. Wilson replied.

After a few minutes of crying to herself, Mildred closed her eyes and thought back to those special times at the Stardust Ballroom. She could remember that they had a lot of great times there.

Once that she and Henry had the kids, they did not go as much as they once did. This was also true of their friends and family. But every month or so, they would hire a babysitter go to dinner and then hit the Stardust Ballroom. Usually they were home about 12:30 or so. Once in a great while they returned at 1 a.m.

Aside from having their children, those were the best times of Mildred's life. Henry and her, would dance the night away, be with friends and then come home and make love.

A half a century later, it was now a distant and rapidly fading memory.

If only she could go back, she thought. If only she could relive those memories and fun times.

If only.

Soon Mildred was disturbed out of her daydream, when Amy, the nurse's assistant returned to check on her.

"How are you doing, Mildred?" Amy asked.

Mildred opened her eyes and looked at her with a sad and lonely smile.

"Are you alright?" Amy asked, a little concerned.

Mildred just quietly nodded and smiled weakly. As much as she liked Amy and her friendly personality, Mildred was upset at being taken away from her daydream.

"Nurse Angela will be in shortly to check your vitals and make sure that you're alright," Amy cheerfully announced.

Soon enough, Nurse Angela Ripley was in to check Mildred's blood pressure, heart rate and overall physical condition.

"Would you like to lie down for your nap?" Nurse Angela asked.

Mildred quietly nodded. She was more than ready to lie down for her daily nap. On top of being physically tired, she was mentally and emotionally spent. It had been an emotionally trying and at times very enjoyable day.

Over the next couple of days, Mildred was visited by each of her children and their spouses. Each one stayed for about an hour and left with varying degrees of frustration and sadness because she could not remember who they were at times.

For each of them the visits were getting shorter in duration and less frequent due to this. She smiled and listened as her children talked but had little recollection of them and who they were talking about with regards to their own children and grandchildren.

"Why do I even visit?" Henry asked as he walked out of the nursing home with his wife, Jane. "She doesn't even know me or you. Why do I visit? I'm a stranger to her."

"Because she's your mother," Jane replied. "And while she may not know who you are, you know who she is. That is why."

Henry squeezed his wife's hand. "Thanks," he said.

"I know what you're going through," Jane commented. "We went through it with my dad, too."

"I know," Henry replied, as they approached their vehicle. "Let's go home."

For Mildred, she knew that some nice people had come to see her, but really had no idea who they were. They claimed to be her children and were kind, and two even looked a little like her late husband Henry but she had no recollection of them.

Her mind drifted back to the times at the Stardust Ballroom.

It was really the only memories that she had left.

On Friday morning, Ruth Morgan went out to buy her sister an anniversary card and a small gift. As she wheeled her car onto the road that led to the store, she was blind-sided by a teenage girl in her car that was texting and driving as she ran a red light. The impact of the accident was on the driver's side of the vehicle and Ruth died instantly from a broken neck and spine.

Ruth never knew what hit her.

For Mildred the anticipation of her anniversary was growing. To the staff of the nursing home, Mildred seemed to be more responsive than she had in some time.

She also seemed to smile more.

Just after lunchtime, Mildred's children all showed up at once to pay her a visit. They felt it was necessary since her sister had just been killed.

"Hi, Mom," Henry said, upon entering her room.

"Hello, Mom," Roger stated.

Lillian went up and kissed the side of her mother's head. "Hi, Mom," she said.

Henry leaned against the wall, while Roger sat in a chair and Lillian finally sat down in the wheelchair.

"Well, how are you doing, Mom? Roger asked. "Are they treating you alright?"

Mildred smiled, and nodded a little. After that there was a long, uncomfortable silence between her and her children where they just looked at each other.

Finally, after a long pregnant pause of silence, Henry spoke. "Look Mom, there is something we have to tell you," he explained. "I am really sorry to tell you this, but your sister Ruth was killed in a car accident this morning. We're really sorry about that but felt that you needed to know."

While she did not speak, this news hit Mildred like a ton of bricks. All she could do was let out was a kind of hoarse gasp. Mildred turned and looked at the photo album on the nightstand, reaching outward for it.

Henry noticed this and moved over to assist. "You want this, Mom?" he asked, referring to the photo album on the nightstand.

Mildred just smiled and nodded.

Henry picked up the photo album and handed it to her. He stood next to her as she opened it up and looked at the picture of Ruth and her husband. "That's aunt Ruth and Uncle Robert!" he exclaimed.

He was soon joined by Roger and Lillian.

"Oh, wow," Lillian said. "It is."

Roger nodded. "Well, she at least can remember some things and people like Aunt Ruth," he stated. "That's good."

"Yeah," Henry agreed.

For the next couple of hours, they kept Mildred company, telling stories about Ruth and their family, much to Mildred's delight. She smiled and her eyes seemed to light up. While she wasn't entirely sure who these people were, they definitely knew Ruth and that meant a lot.

Once they kissed her goodbye and left, Mildred looked at the photo album and began to cry. While she had not remembered everything that her kids had told her, somehow, she already knew that Ruth was gone and would not be visiting her anymore.

The one person who could share the few memories she still had was now dead.

That in itself was terribly heartbreaking to her.

For the rest of the day, Mildred stared out her room window and moped around from the incredible sadness.

That night, Mildred dreamed while she slept. Once again, it was about the Stardust Ballroom. It was the only memory and dream that she had left.

The next day while daydreaming about the Stardust Ballroom, she thought about going to the place where she had so much fun and so many great memories of. It was her singular thought of the whole day. She was going to go to the Stardust Ballroom no matter what and nothing was going to stop her. It was her anniversary and she had to be there.

After dinner, Mildred, while still in her wheelchair, somehow navigated her way out of her room and down the hallway. While the staff noticed her moving, they did not think much of it. The busy and overworked weekend staff somehow did not notice her make her way towards the door. Once at the door, Mildred, using all of her strength and will, stood up and got out of her wheelchair. She then opened the door and left, unnoticed by the staff.

Outside, Mildred knew that the Stardust Ballroom was just over a mile away. She had lived in the area her entire life and somehow still knew the area like the back of her hand.

Weak, tired, and frail, Mildred somehow mustered all her strength to walk the entire distance. Nothing was going to stop her.

While the surrounding area had changed greatly throughout the years, Mildred still knew where the Stardust Ballroom was and how to get there. Mildred was totally oblivious to the winos, as well as the run-down and deserted buildings that she passed along the way. She was driven by a single mind and purpose.

She was going to dance on her anniversary.

When Mildred finally arrived at the Stardust Ballroom, she did not see anybody at first and cautiously opened the door. Once inside, she was greeted by a doorman that everybody knew as Joe. Joe quietly nodded in acknowledgment and let her pass.

Once inside she was greeted by her husband Henry, the love of her life. He kissed her passionately. When she finally pulled away, Mildred noticed that the Stardust Ballroom was dark.

"Happy anniversary, my love," Henry said.

Before she could reply, all of the lights came on at once and everybody yelled "Happy Anniversary!" with confetti and streamers falling all over them.

Mildred began to cry as friends, family and other well-wishers all approached and hugged and kissed them both.

"I knew you would make it," Ruth smiled before hugging her sister. "Happy anniversary."

"Here's a blue corsage for the prettiest girl at the dance," Henry announced, as he placed the corsage on her wrist.

"Okay, everybody!" the bandleader exclaimed. "It's time for the anniversary couple to have the first dance. So, come on out and get the party started, Henry and Mildred Dunlap!"

Henry and Mildred then starting dancing once the band began to play *Stardust.* When the band then started playing *The Tennessee Waltz* afterwards, almost everybody else joined them on the dance floor.

***

It was at this time the medical staff at Autumn Years Nursing Home discovered that Mildred was missing. A search of the premises was then conducted. When she still wasn't found, they contacted the authorities. Amy was called at her home by the medical staff on duty. Initially she couldn't think of anything. Then she thought about what Ruth had told her and how Mildred seemed to remember the Stardust Ballroom and that she possibly wandered over there. The medical staff then called the authorities.

Back at the Stardust Ballroom, it seemed like Mildred had danced and partied for hours. It was just as she remembered it, with everybody laughing, dancing and having an overall great time.

To her, the music and good time seemed to go forever. Or at least she wished it had.

Mildred could not believe how perfect it all was.

When the band slowed down, she and Henry were once again on the center dance floor for what seemed an eternity. Her heart was full, and she was as happy as one ever could be. Or that she had been in quite some time. She closed her eyes and enjoyed living the dream.

***

"So much for a quiet night," Sergeant Steven Burke announced to his partner officer Blake Tillman, outside of a service station.

"What is it?" Tillman asked.

"We have an old lady with dementia walking out of a nursing home and a noise complaint from some houses near the old Stardust Ballroom," Burke explained.

"Really?" Tillman asked. "That place has been deserted for almost forty years."

"Yeah," Burke muttered. "It's probably some kids. Let's go bust up their party at the Stardust first."

"Yeah," Tillman agreed.

A few minutes later the two police officers pulled into the old, weed-filled and cracked pavement of the Stardust Ballroom.

"It looks pretty dark," Tillman commented. "I don't hear anything either."

"Yeah, we better go check it out," Burke muttered, not thrilled about doing so.

After pulling up close to the entrance, both officers got out of the vehicle and proceeded to check out the Stardust Ballroom.

"Call for back-up just in case," Burke ordered.

"Will do," Tillman said.

Burke headed towards the front door. He shined his flashlight on the door. "It's open," he announced, as he pulled out his Glock, readying himself for anything.

Tillman finished calling for back-up and quickly joined his partner.

Once inside they trained their flashlights throughout the place. The old Stardust Ballroom was a shadow of its former self with dilapidated floors and walls, old broken furniture, and other loose debris scattered throughout the entire place.

At first, neither officer saw anything in the dimly-lit, decrepit old dance hall. Then Burke shined his light across the floor and saw what looked like a person lying there in a clump.

"Whoa, wait a minute," Burke announced.

"What the hell?" Tillman asked upon realizing it was a body.

Both officers rushed over to the body that was lying on the floor. Burke crouched down and checked for vitals. There was nothing. No signs of any foul play either.

"She's dead," Burke announced. "She looks to be in her eighties give or take."

"Any I.D.?" Tillman asked.

"Nope," Burke responded. "But I'll bet you dollars to doughnuts that she's the ones who walked out of the nursing home."

"Why would she come here?" Tillman asked. "The place hasn't been opened in years."

"She might not have thought so," Burke added. "She's got smile on her face, a corsage on and here's a strange one, she's got confetti and a streamer on her."

"Well, at least she died happy," Tillman commented. "You would have thought she was partying here. That is strange. Damn strange."

They were soon joined by Sergeant Lee Perry and officer Jim Duncan.

"What do you have?" Perry asked.

"Well, I think we found the missing nursing home lady," Burke replied. "She's dead. No signs of foul play."

"Jim, go call for an ambulance and the CSI crew," Perry ordered. "What about the noise complaint?"

"We've got nothing," Burke responded. "There's no signs of anybody else here. Maybe it was the old lady."

"Maybe," Perry agreed. "She fits the description and the age."

"She probably just died walking here," Burke surmised. "Maybe it was too much for her. The poor thing probably came here hoping it was still open."

"I still wonder why she would come here," Tillman commented.

"She had dementia," Perry replied. "It was probably one of the few things that she could remember. She might have had good memories of the place."

Burke nodded. "That's sad," he muttered. "Poor lady."

"Yeah," Perry agreed.

The officers could hear a siren in the distance getting closer, as they waited for the medical until and CSI team to arrive.

Mildred Dunlap had finally celebrated her anniversary with a last dance at the Stardust Ballroom, just like she'd always wanted.

Mr. Handelman's Bicycle

It had been a rough and trying period of time for Mike Handelman. First, one of his best and oldest friends Robert "Big Bob" Dunleavy had died earlier in the week. They had known each other since Kindergarten and friends just as long. He had just been the latest friend to pass away.

The other trying and personally rough event had been his wife Mary's deteriorating health. She was having heart palpitations, kidney problems and was just diagnosed with the early onset of dementia. She was the love of his life and gradually suffering a little more each day.

Mike was both sad and depressed. It seemed the people that he knew and loved the longest were leaving him. Old age and death had taken far too many of them.

He could deal with the death part. While painful, that was normal. He had been told at a young age by his grandfather that nobody in this life gets out alive. So, that was part of life.

However, with Mary's declining health and now her diagnosis onset of dementia, it was all almost overwhelming to him.

She had been the love of his life ever since they met in elementary school. While now older, in his heart she was still the girl with model-like looks and long blonde hair that was his soulmate. He still found her beautiful.

Now their youth long since faded away and in their

mid-seventies, their bodies were slowly but gradually failing them. Mike knew that was part of the process of life, but it still didn't make it any easier.

On top of that, their three grown children along with their spouses and grandchildren were on them to sell their home of well-over fifty years to move into an assisted living facility or a nursing home.

Both had fought the idea. Now, Mary's diagnosis of the onset of early dementia would once again bring the calls from their adult children, Michael, John and Rebecca and their families to sell their home.

He knew that it was just a matter of time.

"Are you alright?" Mary asked, sensing that her husband was upset.

"Yeah, I suppose so," Mike replied a bit glumly as he drove them home from the doctor's office. "Considering everything."

Mary took a breath and exhaled. "The only thing that really bothers me about this diagnosis is, that I will eventually forget you," she confessed. "You have been the love of my life, Mike, a very fine man and to eventually not recognize you or know who you are after so many wonderful years together is just heartbreaking."

Mike nodded, then reached over with his right hand to hold Mary's left. "I know," he finally said. "We'll get through it somehow. I'll never leave you, ever."

Mary squeezed his hand, with tears welling up in her eyes. "I know," she said, choking back tears. "I know that we'll be fine."

Once home, Mike and Mary went in their house and had lunch. After lunch they both took a nap, as was their almost daily routine.

After their nap, while they were out on their front porch, they were visited by their Robert Dunleavy's son, Robert Jr., whom they always called Bobby.

"Hi Bobby, what brings this visit?" Mike asked, standing up to greet his best friends' son. "Long time, no see."

"Hey there, Mr. Handelman," Bob Dunleavy called out. "My Dad left you something in his will."

"Really?" Mike asked.

"Yeah," Bob replied. "He was adamant about me bringing it over as soon as possible. You were his oldest and best friend and he really wanted you to have it."

"Well, thank you Bobby," Mike said. "That's really kind of you both."

Bob nodded. "Hey, I had some great times growing up with you guys," he stated. "You guys did everything with us kids. Your kids and me went all through school together. We had a great childhood because of you guys. I'm just doing what is right."

"Thank you," Mary said, as she stood up and walked over to her husband.

"It isn't much, but Dad thought you would appreciate it," Bob admitted.

"Thank you," Mike replied.

"I'll be right back," Bob replied. "I need to bring it over."

"Thanks," Mike said, as he watched Bob go back to his now deceased friend's old house to retrieve what he had bequeathed to him in his will.

A few minutes later Bob returned, pushing a bicycle. It was not just any bicycle but a 1953 Schwinn Black Phantom.

"Oh, my God," Mike gasped, recognizing what it was immediately.

"Wow," Mary muttered.

'I'm not sure what it was, but Dad kept it in mint condition," Bob explained. "He kept it covered up and hidden. He taped an envelope to the handlebars. Do you know what it is?"

"It's a vintage 1953 Schwinn Black Phantom," Mike announced as he approached Bob and the bike. "We both got one when we were 12 years old. We rode all over the place. We spent the entire summer riding them. I don't think there was a place we didn't go without them. Boy, it sure takes me back to my youth."

"Dad said it would," Bob replied. "He said that you would appreciate it."

"Oh, I do," Mike said, as he hugged Bob. "Thank you."

"You're welcome, Mr. Handleman," Bob replied, hugging him back. He then hugged Mary as well. "Well, I have to go back and help David and Tom and our wives continue to sort through his stuff. So, if you'll excuse me."

"Anytime," Mike responded, waving at Bob.

"Wow, that must be worth some money," Mary observed. "It looks like it just left the factory."

"It sure does," Mike agreed.

"Just don't expect either of us to ride it," Mary commented. "I don't think either of our hips could take a fall at our age."

Mike just quietly nodded.

"Don't forget to open the letter," Mary said, reminding Mike.

"I will," Mike replied. "Let me put it in the garage first," Mike replied.

"Okay," Mary sighed, knowing that Mike was still choked up over his friend's death and inheritance.

She knew that he needed to be alone when he read the letter by himself first. He always had internalized a lot of things. Even though she was the one with deteriorating health, Mary worried about Mike's outlook and health as well.

Once inside the garage, Mike carefully removed the

taped envelope from the bike, then gently opened it and then began reading.

Mike-

If you are reading this, then my time has come, and I am no longer around.

It has been great knowing you and Mary all of these years. A guy couldn't ask for a better friend. You are as much a brother to me as a friend.

Tell Mary that Carol and I loved every minute that we spent together, whether it was playing cards, picnics with our kids or just hanging out talking. It was all great.

Anyway, I left you this bike. I know it will take you back to the days of our youth. I found it at a garage sale while some man's kid was selling it after he died. He said his father didn't get a chance to ride it before he just suddenly passed away. He was selling it for a hundred bucks, and I just had to have it.

It is in mint condition and almost magical.

So, old buddy, please take a spin on the old Black Phantom. I rode it a couple of times when no one was around and found that I had bought more than I had originally bargained for. You will find that out for yourself when you take it for a spin.

It can take you to places you won't believe. I would have taken Carol on it, but she passed away before I could. After that I just couldn't do it. I missed her too bad and maybe did not have the guts. But it will definitely take you back.

Trust me on this.

You may never want to get off or come back from the experience.

Enjoy the days of your youth again. Take Mary with you. It's a real experience.

Love, your brother,

"Big" Bob

Tears welled up in Mike's eyes. He rubbed them, took

a deep breath and parked the bike in a corner of his garage.

Mike wondered what his friend meant by riding the bike will take him back to the days of his youth. He seriously doubted it with the way his knees had been for the last twenty years.

Mike was a bit perplexed. Bob had been a pretty rational man. He always had been and wasn't one to overreact. He stared at the bike, shaking his head. He had to seriously think about this.

When Mike returned, he showed Mary the letter which made her break down and cry.

"That is so sweet," she said between sobs, and managing to smile somehow.

"Yeah," Mike agreed.

"What do you think he means?" Mary asked, as she finally stopped crying.

"I don't really know," Mike admitted. "I'm trying to figure that out.

"Maybe he was losing it at the time he wrote this," Mary suggested.

"I don't think so, honey," Mike countered. "Bob was pretty level-headed and rational all the way up until the end. I really don't think so."

"Not to change the subject, but when do we tell the kids about my diagnosis?" Mary asked. "They really should know."

"I think we should hold off for as long as possible," Mike replied. "I really do not want to hear how we need to sell our home and belongings to move into some assisted living place just yet."

"To tell you the truth, I really don't either," Mary admitted. "I'd like to stay in our home for as long as possible. It's where our life has been."

The next couple of days were both hectic and

tumultuous for Mike and Mary. Mary had to be taken into emergency. Her kidneys were worsening and the lining to her bladder was deteriorating, along with other minor ailments.

In emergency, Mike and Mary's adult children all showed up concerned when she was placed in a room.

"Dad, can we talk to you?" their son Michael asked.

"Yeah, sure," Mike replied, patting his son's shoulder. "Let's go outside the room, though."

They were joined by their other children, John and Rebecca, while Michael and John's wives kept Mary company. Michael and John looked almost exactly like Mike did when he was in his mid-to-late forties, tall and lean with slightly graying hair while Rebecca was the spitting image of Mary with long golden hair and similar height and physical build.

"Look, Dad, I think you and Mom really need to consider an assisted living place," Michael started. "It would be for the best."

"I know you think that," Mike replied. "But we're not ready for that just yet. We're not ready to give up our independence."

"But Dad, you guys are needing some help," John added. "You're both having a hard time taking care of each other now."

"We get by," Mike politely protested.

"Dad, you and Mom can't keep doing this," Rebecca countered. "She's getting worse and you're doing nothing."

Mike did his best to not get angry. "That's not true," he argued. "I take her to the doctors and her tests. We do everything they tell us to do."

"So, you're just going to stay in that house and wait," Michael snapped.

"Look, I know you're a lawyer and have connections,

but we don't want any of that yet," Mike said. "That home has been ours for over fifty years. We raised a family in it. We're trying to hold on as long as possible until the time comes."

"Okay," Michael muttered.

"Just give us more time," Mike pleaded. "Let us say goodbye to our home our own way and when think it is right."

"Alright," Michael said. "But if Mom gets worse, we've agreed that we might have to take matters into our own hands to help you guys."

Mike nodded. "That almost sounds like a threat," he replied, with a tone a seriousness in his voice.

"It's not," John responded. "It's that we're concerned. We just love you guys and are very concerned."

Tears welled up in Rebecca's eyes. "Dad, we just want what is best for you and Mom, that's all," she sobbed. "We love you."

Mike went in and hugged Rebecca. "I know," he said. "Come here you two." Michael and John moved in closer to be hugged by their father. "I love you guys, but you have to let us really think about it. We're not ruling it out, but we do need some time."

"Okay," Michael muttered.

"Okay, for now," John agreed. "We can set aside this conversation for now, but we will have to address it sometime."

All Mike could do was nod. He knew that neither he nor Mary wanted this. At least not right now.

Mary spent a couple of days in the hospital before she was finally released.

Once home from the hospital, Mary was still weak and frail. Mike carefully helped her up the few steps that led to their house.

"Where do you want to go?" Mike asked. "Which room?"

"I'd like to lay down," Mary responded. "You know what they say about hospitals, they wake you up to give you sleeping pills there."

"Yeah," Mike laughed nervously.

It was good that Mary still had her sense of humor, he thought. She usually could find something humorous in a trying situation.

Once inside, Mike helped her to the bedroom, where she was safely lying in bed and comfortable.

While Mary was asleep, Mike went out to his garage. He needed time to think and tinker with something as a distraction. As he was about to work on some small project, the 1953 Schwinn Black Phantom caught his eye.

He wondered about the things Bob wrote in the letter. He then figured the only way to find out was to actually ride the bike. After some trepidation and hesitation, he decided to do it. Fortunately for him he and Mary both rode a tandem bicycle only a couple of years ago, so riding a bike now wouldn't be that much trouble for him.

Mike opened up his garage door and walked the bike to his doorway. He then lifted up the kickstand and climbed on. As he started peddling, he found the ride was nice and smooth and easy. Riding it came back to him as if it were yesterday.

Mike decided to take it for a longer spin and started riding further down the block. He was lost in riding the bicycle. He felt young again.

The further down the road he went, the more things seemed to change. They were different but had a kind of familiarity to them. As he peddled the bike closer to his old neighborhood the scenery began to change. Soon the street that he lived on looked nothing like it did currently.

It looked like it had years earlier.

A small farmers' market and cottage were now in the place of the strip mall that had eventually replaced them. The road also narrowed. The new houses that encroached on some of the stately old manors were now just memories.

As Mike continued to peddle, his surroundings looked as if they had years earlier.

At one point, Mike was almost afraid to stop because he was uncertain what would happen. So, he kept riding. He decided to keep going towards the area where he had grown up. Unfortunately, with time, a few of the houses were deserted and empty while others were run down and not kept up. Minutes later, he found himself on his old street. The strangest thing of all, it now looked like it did when he was younger.

Much younger.

Finally, he came to an abrupt stop. Mike could not believe what he was seeing. Somehow, he had gone back to the days of his youth. Mike looked down at his hands and noticed that the sunspots and wrinkles were no longer there either. Mike looked in the window of a 1949 Dodge Deluxe Sedan and saw his reflection. He was young. Mike saw that he was about 12 or 13 years old.

"Oh, my God," he muttered in disbelief, looking around.

He then saw some kids playing in one of the lots near one of the houses. Mike knew by sight who they all were.

"Oh, my God!" he exclaimed. "That's Mikey and Bobby Hegan! That's Teddy Baxter and Donnie Simmons! Oh, wow!"

Tears welled up in his eyes. These were the same guys that he and Bob Dunleavy had grown up with and played with daily. A flood of memories came flowing back to him and were almost overwhelming. He watched as old Mr.

Simmons polished his '49 Buick and Mr. Hegan ducked and dodged his water sprinkler while trying to move it.

"My God, I'm back," he muttered. "I'm back home to my childhood." Mike looked down at the bicycle. "So, that's what Bob meant in his letter. You really can take me back."

Mike decided that he had better head back home to Mary. Deep down, he did not want to go back but knew he had to. For a moment he wondered if he could, but then decided that it must be possible, since Bob came back.

Mike turned around and peddled back home. The nearer to home he got the more his surroundings looked like the present day. Soon, he was back home.

Mike was still filled with a sense of shock and disbelief. He was also somewhat fatigued by his bike ride but also felt good and a bit invigorated by it as well.

He was extremely uncertain about whether to tell Mary about his experience. He might think he was delusional. But then again, she always had a way of knowing when he was serious as well. If anybody would believe him, it would be Mary.

Mike returned the bike back to his garage, then locked the door. He looked down the block wondering if what he experienced really did happen. Shaking his head, he finally went back inside.

Once inside, he found Mary awake, sitting in her chair, watching television and knitting. "So, where did you go?" she asked.

"For a ride," Mike replied.

"A ride?" Mary asked.

"Yeah, I tried out Bob's old bike," Mike admitted. "I took it for a little spin."

"You what?" Mary asked, somewhat annoyed. "Aren't you a little old to be doing that? You could have fallen and hurt yourself."

"Probably," Mike answered. "I just thought I'd try it out and see, that's all. I just thought I would take it out for a spin."

"So, how was it?" Mary asked, her momentary anger starting to dissipate.

"It was something else," Mike replied. "The ride was as smooth and fun as I remembered it being. It took me back in more ways than I could believe."

"Well, just be careful," Mary warned. "We don't need you falling and breaking a hip you, old fool. So, the bike took you back, huh?"

"In more ways than you can imagine," Mike responded.

"Okay," Mary said, not quite certain about his response.

"I'm sorry if I upset you," Mike apologized.

"I'm sorry for snapping at you," Mary responded. "I was just concerned."

"I know," Mike stated. "It's been tough lately.

The next day while Mary was once again taking a nap after lunch, Mike took the bike out. Just like before as he peddled down the street the scenery began to change, and he went back in time. Once again, he was a youth watching the boys he knew as a kid.

"Hey, Mikey!" yelled a distantly familiar voice. "Light a fire under it!"

"Huh?" Mike grunted, momentarily confused.

Mike turned and looked, seeing that it was his old neighbor and friend, Timmy Douglas.

"Come on man!" Timmy yelled. "The guys are all riding down to the river! We gotta catch up to them!"

"Oh, okay!" Mike replied, finally remembering that he was young again.

Mike road alongside of Timmy as they eventually

caught up to the other guys. He was thrilled to see the old guys from the neighborhood. After an unsuccessful for hunt for pollywogs and other aquatic creatures, the boys decided to ride to some nearby field where they played everything from hide and seek, to just plain rolling down some of the grassy knolls of the field.

Mike couldn't remember having a better time. At least like this and in quite some time. After a while, he realized that he had been gone for quite some time and needed to get back to Mary.

"Hey guys, I gotta go," he announced and peddled back home to the present time.

Once home he put the bike inside his garage and went inside.

"Did you enjoy your ride?" Mary asked.

"Yes, Mary, I did," Mike replied. "It was great."

"Where exactly do you go?" Mary asked.

"I rode around a bit and back to the old neighborhood," Mike replied. "It takes me back in time and I reminisce."

"Really?" Mary asked, a bit skeptical of Mike's answer.

"Yes, Mary really," Mike replied.

"Okay, but I feel like there is something you are not telling me about the trips," Mary commented.

Mike nodded, then took a deep breath and exhaled. "Mary, there is something magical about the bike," he responded. "The bike takes me back. I mean *actually* takes me back. I mean *literally* back to my youth. I see people, old friends and people we used to know. It's really something."

"I love you, honey but do you realize how delusional that sounds?" Mary asked, rhetorically. "I mean, come on."

"Don't you think I know that?" Mike asked in response. "Why do you think I was hesitant to tell you? I hardly believe it myself. But, it's true. As unbelievable as it sounds it is true."

Mary looked at Mike handily. He had always been up front and honest with her about everything. She began to wonder if he too wasn't suffering from the early onset of dementia or just unable to deal with reality anymore. Worse she began to fear for his sanity.

"I don't mean to be this way, Mike but ever since you started riding the bike, you have been acting different," Mary stated.

"It's only been a couple of times," Mike protested. "Maybe I act differently because I did experience those things on the bike."

"Well, let me know first," Mary snapped. "I woke up and you were gone again. At least have the courtesy to tell me first."

"Okay, Mary, I at least owe you that," Mike stated. "I will do that."

For the rest of the day and into the evening they made small talk but did not broach the subject of the bike. Even when they kissed goodnight, Mike felt like Mary was growing more distant and uncertain of him. However even if she was, Mike decided to continue riding the bike.

He needed it.

The next few weeks, Mike's bike trips became longer and more frequent. While not entirely pleased, Mary could tell that Mike's overall demeanor and health seemed to improve. While she did not believe him about the bike trips taking him back to his youth, she had no complaints about it either.

She did mention it in passing to her daughter Rebecca and her sons, John and Michael, when they called to see how she and Mike were doing.

When Mike arrived back from one of his trips, he was greeted by an inquisitive and perturbed Michael.

"Dad, where have you been?" he asked as his father wheeled his bike up to the garage.

"Riding, why?" Mike asked.

"Are you sure that's smart at your age," Michael asked.

"Probably not," Mike responded, as he pushed the bike into his garage. "But it's fun and I enjoy it."

"Mom told us that you actually believe it takes you back in time," Michael commented. "What the hell is that? You believe it actually takes you back in time? Are you kidding?"

"Yes," Mike responded.

"You're living in make-believe, Dad," Michael commented. "Do you realize how ridiculous that sounds?"

"Look son, I don't know what to say," Mike added. "I don't know what else to tell you. The more I ride, the further back I go."

"Oh, my God," Michael snapped, shaking his head. "I can't believe you. First Mom has been diagnosed with dementia and now you're showing signs of it. It's just a damned bicycle, not a time machine. I'm sorry Dad, but I think you're losing it."

"Now just a damned minute," Mike roared back at his son. "I do not have dementia, nor have I lost my mind. You can believe me or not believe me, but I will not be talked to like I am some child or a senile old coot."

Michael shook his head. "Dad, you cannot keep doing this," he argued. "Mom's upset and so are we. You sound like you're not dealing in reality. John, Rebecca, and I think it's time you both went into a nursing home or an assisted living facility. In fact, we're quite adamant about it."

"Really?" Mike asked. "You act like we do not have a say in it. I don't think we're ready and we would consider it when the time came."

"Dad, we believe that time is now," Michael insisted. "We cannot have you ride all over Hell's half acre as Mom is deteriorating in front of your eyes. We just can't."

Mike locked the garage door. He was not thrilled. "So, this is some kind of ultimatum?" he asked.

Michael took a deep breath then exhaled. "I'm afraid it is," he admitted.

"Over my dead body," Mike snapped. "I think you had better leave."

"Okay, Dad," Michael stated. "But this isn't over. We will be back. I already have the paperwork ready for you both. You will both be well-cared for."

Michael headed for his car, waved, got in and abruptly left. Mike knew there was more in store for them. He looked up and saw Mary outside crying. At first, he felt a sense of betrayal by her, but then realized that he wouldn't have believed his story either.

"I'm so sorry." she sobbed. "I didn't mean for this to happen. I don't want to go in any home. At least not right now."

Mike looked at her, walked over to her, and held her gently as she continued crying. She had always been a pretty little thing, and now she felt frail and almost breakable.

"I know honey, I know," he said. "Neither do I."

"Michael admitted to me that they had us declared unable to care for ourselves, and need full-time care," Mary explained between sobs. "He said that he had the paperwork completed."

Mike was angry and hurt. "Oh, God," he muttered.

"I can't remember everything he said," Mary cried. "I wish I could, but it was all legalistic mumbo-jumbo."

"It's alright," Mike said, trying to comfort Mary. "It's alright. As long as we are together, we'll be alright."

After a while Mary stopped crying. He could almost understand his kids' reasoning for what they were planning and doing but was hurt that they didn't do it in a better way. He felt they could have at least respected their wishes, better than they had.

That night they were lying in bed, both struggling with trying to sleep.

"You asleep?" Mary asked.

"No," Mike answered.

"What do you think we should do?" Mary asked.

"I don't know," Mike replied. "I need to try and sleep on it before I can really think. I need sleep and rest. I can't think when I'm tired."

"Goodnight," Mary said.

"Goodnight," Mike replied.

Finally, after several minutes of just lying there, Mike and Mary were able to drift off to sleep. Once asleep Mike began to dream.

He began to dream about Mary when she was younger, more vibrant and in her '20s. He thought about her long blonde hair, curvaceous and shapely, yet lean body. She was the most beautiful woman he had ever laid eyes on...ever. He then dreamed of the first time they made love. Like the bicycle he had just been given it was magical and he was under her loving spell forever.

Even now, in spite of her advancing age, he still found her beautiful.

As Mike continued to dream about Mary in her youth, the idea came to him. She needed to get on the bike and go back with him. He needed to take her. They both needed to go and stay there.

Mike woke up from his dreaming. "That's it!" he exclaimed sitting up and accidently waking up Mary.

Mary sat up and looked at him strangely. She did not appear to recognize him at first. "What's it?" she finally asked.

"Mary are you alright?" he asked. She did not answer at first. "Mary? Mary? Are you alright?"

Finally, after a few moments she responded. "Yes, I'm alright. What's the matter Mike?"

"Nothing," he replied. "Nothing. Nothing at all. Let's go back to sleep."

Mary finally nodded then laid back down. Mike knew that she just had an episode. He also knew that they would get worse and more frequent. Mike knew what he had to do. Or more like what they had to do.

After lunch tomorrow they would do what needed to be done.

After breakfast the next morning, Mike decided to broach the subject with Mary.

"I have an idea on what we can do," Mike announced.

"About what?" Mary asked.

Mike could see that she was a little confused. "You know our kids wanting to put us in a nursing home or an assisted living facility?"

"Oh, oh, yeah, that's right," Mary said, finally recalling the memory. "What's your idea?"

"After a few essential chores around here, I will show you," Mike explained. "But you have to trust me on this."

Mary nodded. "I do," she said. "I really do."

"Good," Mike replied. "It's the only thing I can think of. I just hope it works."

"I am sure it will," Mary stated. "Whatever it is, I am sure it will."

After their conversation, Mike pulled out the will that he and Mary had notarized and recorded. He looked it over. All three children were to get equal shares of their properties. It was pretty cut and dried. He then placed it on the dining room table where they could easily find it. Mike then made sure other legal documents and legal papers were also easily found as well, placing them next to the will.

By the time he was finished, it was going on noon.

He then fixed Mary and himself a light lunch. In the middle of lunch, the phone rang. It was Michael. Mike answered then listened as Michael explained what they were planning. "Okay," Mike said, before hanging up the phone.

"Who was that?" Mary asked.

"It was Michael," Mike announced. "The kids are coming over. I guess the kids are coming over. I think they want to prevent a united front when giving us their ultimatum."

"Oh," Mary muttered. "So, what's your plan?"

Mike led Mary out to the driveway. He then went in and brought out the 1953 Schwinn Black Phantom.

Mary looked confused. "What are you going to do with that?" she asked.

Mike then climbed on. He beckoned for Mary to join him. She could sit on the book carrier part above the rear tire. "Get on," he ordered. "We're going for a spin. So, hold on tight."

Mary was hesitant, but eventually decided to join him. "Okay," she said, before climbing on and holding on tight to Mike. "Where are we going?"

"Back," Mike replied, as he started peddling the bike. "We're going back."

At first Mike struggled to get going with two of them on the bike. But after a few yards he managed to get going at a pretty good speed.

As they headed down the street, they passed their children and their spouses in their vehicles heading towards their house. All their vehicles came to screeching halts in order to avoid from hitting the vehicle in front of them.

Mike saw them and began to peddle harder as the cars tried to maneuver to turn around. They soon heard the sounds of police sirens getting closer as well. By the time their kids were able to turn their vehicles around to pursue their parents, Mike was a couple of hundred yards ahead of them. He figured that Michael must have called the police on them.

Mike was tired and sore from peddling so hard, but knew if they stopped now, they were doomed. He also knew that the cars were getting closer.

"Keep holding tight!" Mike exclaimed.

Mary held onto Mike tighter. The further they rode, Mary began to notice that the area was changing. Places they passed began to look like they once had. Places that were long gone were now back in place.

Soon they were not only being pursued by their children's vehicles but by the authorities as well. Mike looked back and could see they were gaining on them. The two-hundred-yard gap was now much less.

Mike knew that he only had a few more yards to go before reaching the outskirts of the old area. The area where he first met Mary. With their pursuers only about fifty yards behind them, Mike turned down the street where he first saw Mary.

As they turned down the street, Mary noticed that the wrinkles in her hands were gone and her long flowing golden blond locks were back. Mary realized that she had somehow gone back to her late teens or early twenties.

"Stop!" she yelled.

Mike peddled a little further before stopping. He got off the bike, turned around and saw Mary was young and beautiful again, like she was when they first met. Mary was astounded to see that Mike was looking tall, muscular and viral like he had been when she first laid eyes on him as well.

By the time children's vehicles and police turned the corner, there was nobody in front of them. It was as if their parents had disappeared, almost right in front of their eyes. They had been only about thirty yards ahead of them when after turning a corner they were gone.

Michael stopped his car and got out. John and Rebecca followed suit. They stood outside of their cars in shock and disbelief along with their spouses.

"Where did they go?" John asked.

"We'll continue to search for them," the police officer announced. "They couldn't have gotten far, given their ages."

"Please do," Michael said. "We need to find them, so they don't get hurt."

"Where did they go," John asked again.

"I have no idea," Michael replied.

"Maybe, just maybe, Dad was telling the truth," Rebecca commented. "Maybe that bike really did take him back."

Michael and John looked at Rebecca and then down the street in wonderment.

"Well, wherever they are I hope they're happy," John stated.

"I'm sure they are," Rebecca responded, with tears welling up in her eyes. "They're together. So, I know they're happy."

Michael nodded, took a deep breath and exhaled, with tears welling up in his eyes. "I think you're right," he admitted. "Maybe this just worked out for the best. I'd prefer to lose them this way than to old age."

"Here, here to that," John agreed. "Good for Mom and Dad. Let's go back to the house and then get some dinner. We have got some planning to do."

Mary looked around in astonishment as she and Mike returned to their younger days when he courted her.

"Wow!" Mary exclaimed. "Now I know what Bob's letter meant. The bike really does take you back. We're young again."

"Yeah," Mike agreed as he moved closer and began to embrace her. "When I first came back, I didn't want to leave, but I couldn't stay here without you."

Mary smiled coyly. "I love you," she said. "We've got a lot of lovemaking to make up for the past few years and an eternity to do it. So, kiss me you young, old fool."

A Condition of the Skin

The flames burned high into the nighttime sky, each flame licking the darkness as it came off of the twenty-foot burning cross that stood in the clearing against the cypress trees of the bayou. The burning cross and a number of hand-held torches illuminated the area almost as well as gaslights in the city.

Standing in white robes and hoods were the self-ordained protectors of white supremacy and purity was the local Ku Klux Klan, as they stood assembled and ready to dole out their vigilante justice in the name of keeping the order of things as they were.

At the head of the formation of cruel hatred and bigotry stood Colonel William McMasters, a Civil War hero, local legend, owner of a lot of property in the area and worse of all, the Grand Dragon. McMasters, a middle-aged man with graying hair and mustache, stood watching his fellow Klansmen standing in an almost military formation.

He watched coldly as four of his largest men half-dragged a beaten and bloodied black middle-aged man named Taurean LeDeau down the center aisle of the formation of white-sheeted hatemongers.

Tried as he did to resist and protest, it was all in futility. Any resistance Taurean LeDeau put up was met with fists, clubs and bootheels. After a while it was all Taurean LeDeau could do to remain conscious, let alone stand.

Once he was brought before Colonel McMasters, the Grand Dragon and his lieutenants next to him, Taurean LeDeau stood glaring through his one good, unswollen and unblackend eye, while being subdued by his larger captors.

There was a long, uneasy silence that hung in the air as the Grand Dragon of the Klan and Taurean LeDeau looked directly at each other unflinchingly. Both men stared daggers at the other with neither one giving an inch mentally in spite of the differing circumstances.

Colonel McMasters took a deep breath and exhaled. "You have been brought before us because of accusations of practicing voodoo, inciting the local negro populations and the touching of a white woman," he announced coldly. "Are you not the one known as Taurean Ledeau?"

LeDeau nodded quietly.

"Answer the colonel!' exclaimed one of the larger men next to him as he struck LeDeau in the side, causing him to fall to his knees in pain.

After a few moments LeDeau managed to get back to his feet, seething in pain, and trying to catch his breath. "Yes," he finally muttered hoarsely. "I am Taurean LeDeau."

"You have been found guilty of all these things," McMasters continued. "Do you have anything to say for yourself before sentence is pronounced?"

LeDeau looked directly at McMasters, his anger remaining in check, but still obviously there. "Would it do any good?" he asked in a thick Creole accent. "You will do what you want regardless of what I say or do."

Colonel McMasters pursed his lips and nodded. "You're much more perceptive than I thought," he finally admitted. "For a negro, you're very intelligent. Maybe too smart for your own good."

Taurean just glared at McMasters with his one good

eye. "You underestimate me, Colonel McMasters," he snapped, with his thick Creole accent. "You like to play God with men's lives. You…"

It was then that one of the larger men hit LeDeau across the left side of his face, knocking him to the ground, dazing him. "We'll have quite enough of that, boy!" the big Klansman growled.

"Imagine that, a heathen voodoo priest, talking about God," McMasters chuckled, which caused a number of the other Klansmen to snicker and laugh as well.

After a few moments, LeDeau was able to get back on his feet, staring defiantly at the Grand Dragon.

Colonel McMaster's nodded, "I shall pronounce sentence," he announced. "You, Taurean LeDeau shall be hung by the neck until dead for your crimes."

LeDeau began to recite an incantation in Creole and Cajun that none of the men could understand.

"It's a good thing you're saying your prayers, LeDeau," McMasters commented. "You'll need them where you're going, boy."

"They're not prayers, Colonel," LeDeau warned. "It was a curse upon you."

McMasters was momentarily taken aback. Before he could respond, LeDeau broke free from his captors, tackling Colonel McMasters. He grabbed the colonel's left arm just above his wrist so tightly that it felt like a vice clamping around it even through his white robe and shirt.

The four large Klansmen finally grabbed LeDeau, beating him unmercifully to a bloody pulp before he let go of McMasters' left arm.

"Get your hands off of the colonel, you filthy nigger!" one of the larger Klansmen spat.

By the time they had finished with him, LeDeau was barely conscious and now had his hands bound behind his back. Colonel McMasters was helped off the ground by the others. He was angry and disturbed by what had just happened.

Finally regaining his composure and rubbing his left arm, McMasters glared at LeDeau. "String him up!" he barked. "Any last words, LeDeau?"

LeDeau's head drooped as he was only partially conscious.

"I suppose not," one of McMaster's Klan lieutenant remarked.

Finally, after a moment or two, LeDeau was able to raise his head and utter through his battered and bloodied lips in his thick Creole accent. "You shall become what you hate, Colonel. Mark my words, you shall become what you hate!" He then roared with an almost maniacal laughter.

For a moment McMasters was taken aback and frightened, but quickly regained himself. "String him up, boys!" he ordered.

The four larger Klansmen dragged LeDeau over to a large solitary oak tree in the clearing, one that had been used for lynching many times before. Another Klansman had already thrown a rope with a noose over a large branch. LeDeau was then seated on a horse as the noose was placed around his neck. LeDeau was still laughing at the colonel. After a few seconds, the horse's rear was slapped, and he was hanged.

He struggled for a few seconds against the tightening ropes as his life slipped away into the night. As soon as he stopped struggling, another Klansman shot him in the back of the head with a Winchester rifle.

Once LeDeau was dead, there were celebratory cries and cheers amongst the Klan members. In their hate-filled state, they managed to destroy another human being that was not like them.

As they celebrated, McMasters rubbed his sore, aching

left forearm that LeDeau had grabbed earlier.

"Well, we rid ourselves of that one," Jesse Devereaux, the second in command of the Klan spat defiantly. "You alright, Sir?"

"Yes," McMasters responded. "On both counts."

"I think you may have been too lenient or easy on him," Devereaux continued. "He should have never been able to touch you. We should have just burned his shack down with him in it."

"I think you might be right there," McMasters agreed, still rubbing his throbbing left arm. "Either way, he's dead now."

Both men watched as the twenty-foot cross continued to burn as the others all cheered and celebrated, drinking and shooting off their firearms.

While it had been a relief to get rid of Taurean LeDeau, something still troubled McMasters. The words that LeDeau had muttered about him becoming what he hated kept echoing in his ears. When one of his underlings passed him a bottle of bourbon, McMasters took big drink. McMasters needed it. He then passed the bottle back.

For the white-sheeted hate-mongers it was a long night of festivities and celebration. They had finally rid themselves of the person that had bedeviled them of late.

By the time McMasters arrived home it was late. He greeted his deceased wife Hannah's portrait like he always did whether leaving or arriving home. It was in the wee hours of the morning when he finally was able to go to bed. Exhausted, sleep came very easily to him.

By the time he woke up, it was well after nine a.m. Still a bit tired and groggy, he forced himself out of bed. He felt as if he already missed too much of the day.

As McMasters started to get dressed, he once again felt a twinge of pain in his left arm. He rubbed it, hoping that it would cause the pain to subside. Finally, after minute or two of rubbing, he looked down at his arm.

There, in the center of his left arm, was an innocuous little brown dot. It looked like a freckle or mole. Still, McMasters thought it had not been there before. He wasn't certain of it, but he hadn't noticed it earlier.

He figured it was just him getting older. He definitely wasn't a young man anymore. He was bound to have some wrinkles, age spots, moles and freckles.

He quickly dressed and thought no more of it.

McMasters knew that he had a full day ahead of him and needed to get going. After breakfast he had his stable boy, Dean Frederickson, ready his horse Alexander for him to ride into town and check on his business, McMasters Mercantile.

Once in town he was greeted by a number of familiar faces, a number of which that were with him the night before. Many of the greetings were quiet nods, a tip of the cap and even a salute or two. McMasters politely returned the courtesy, like a good Southern gentleman would do.

The times may have changed with the end of the Civil War, but *he* was not about to, even if his side was defeated. Some things were just not going to change. That included keeping the negro in his place even if he wasn't a slave anymore. As far as McMasters was concerned there would be no "uppity negroes" anywhere near his town as long as he was alive.

When he finally arrived at his business he was greeted by his store's manager, Archer Wainright. "Good morning, Colonel. How are you today, Sir?"

"Very well," McMasters replied.

"Business is a little slow this morning," Wainright reported. "I expect it will pick up soon."

"Good, good," McMasters said, looking through the ledger for the week.

It was then that McMasters felt a twinge in his arm again that caused him to wince a bit.

"You alright, Sir?" Wainright asked.

"Yes," McMasters replied. "I think I injured my arm last night."

"Oh,"

"I might pay Doc Wentworth a visit," McMasters continued. "He'll probably give me a bottle of liniment for it. Carry on with the good work, Archer."

"Yes, Sir."

McMasters decided to pay Doc Wentworth a visit about his arm.

"Ever since that damned nigger grabbed me last night, it's been aching," he thought. *"He probably just bruised it real good."*

Once McMasters arrived at Doc Wentworth's office, he found him leaning back in his chair smoking a large Cuban cigar. Doc Wentworth was much older than McMasters. In his seventies, he had a face like wrinkled leather under a snow-white beard.

"William!" Wentworth exclaimed. "What brings this visit?"

"Well, Doc, I think I might have injured my arm last night," McMasters went on to explain.

Doc thought for a minute, then realized where the colonel was and what he'd been doing last night. "Really?" he finally responded. "Well, let me take a look at it then."

Doctor Wentworth kept his cigar in his mouth as McMasters removed his coat and rolled up his sleeve. As Wentworth examined the arm, he pressed it and move it to see if it was broken.

"It doesn't always hurt," McMasters explained. "It just gets a painful twinge in it every so often."

"Hmmm," Wentworth muttered, as he continued to examine the arm. "So, what happened exactly?'

"My arm was grabbed pretty hard by someone,"

McMasters replied.

"It could be bruised under the skin," Wentworth opined. "You could have somehow strained the muscle. Let me give you some liniment to rub on it. Do it twice a day. Once in the morning and once in the evening."

"Alright," McMasters replied. "What do I owe you?"

"Two bits," Wentworth answered, as he went to retrieve a bottle of liniment. He soon returned with the bottle, handing it to McMasters. "Here."

"Thanks, Doc," McMasters said, taking the liniment bottle from him. "Two bits, huh? Isn't that the same price as a bottle of whiskey?"

"Do tell," Wentworth responded, with a large grin on his face.

By the time McMasters arrived home he was exhausted. The events of the night before and today's business dealings had taken their toll on him. He ate dinner that his housekeeper Alma Ledbetter made for him, then retired for the evening.

As McMasters undressed for bed, he noticed that the mark on his left arm had increased in size. It now looked twice as large as it had earlier. Figuring it was bruised, he rubbed Doc Wentworth's liniment on it, then went to bed.

While he slept, McMasters dreamed of the events from the night before. He repeatedly kept coming back to LeDeau's warning and his maniacal laughter. He then dreamed that it was LeDeau that was hanging *him*, instead of the way that it had been.

At that point, McMasters woke up screaming in the middle of the night. "Dear, God," he muttered, shaking and rubbing his face after the horrific dream.

After a few minutes, he finally settled down enough to go back to sleep.

When morning arrived, McMasters did not feel rested. He was still tired. As he washed up for the morning, he noticed mark on his arm had grown significantly. It was now the size of a silver dollar. He figured it was either more bruising or from the Doc's liniment. It also no longer seemed to ache like it once had.

Still, he was a bit troubled by brown mark's growing in size. He was not thrilled about it.

McMasters dressed and went about his daily chores and business. He liked to stay busy. For in his mind, idle hands were the Devil's workshop. The next couple of days were a flurry of activity for McMasters. He had been kept so busy the days were almost a blur to him. Over those couple of days, he had not paid much attention to brown spot on his arm.

When he woke up on the third day and started to wash up, he looked down to see that the spot had now grown to the size of a grapefruit. This greatly troubled him. He stopped using the liniment immediately, thinking that was what might have caused the brown mark to grow.

McMasters quickly got dressed, wolfed down breakfast and headed straight into town to Dr. Wentworth's office. He had to see him. He was more than a little upset and frightened by this condition.

When Wentworth finally examined his arm, he was taken aback by it as well. He examined it with his glasses on. He touched and squeezed it, perplexed at what it was exactly. "Well, it seems to have grown," he finally muttered. "Does it hurt at all?"

"No," McMasters replied. "Do you have any idea what it is?"

"Well, it doesn't appear to be any kind of infection," Wentworth continued. "Have you had any fevers, or any other health issues at all lately?"

"No, Doc," McMasters responded. "Nothing."

"It could be some kind of condition of the skin," Wentworth concluded. "What exactly, I don't know. It could just be temporary. In all honesty I'm not at all certain of what it is."

"Can you do anything for it?" McMasters asked.

"Let me look in my medical journals," Wentworth replied. "I need a few days. Come back next Monday. Hopefully, I should have something for you then."

"Thanks, Doc," McMasters said. "What do I owe?"

"Nothing," Wentworth replied. "At least not yet. Not until I can really do something for you."

"Alright," McMasters muttered. "I will see you Monday."

McMasters left Doctor Wentworth's office even more upset and concerned than he was before. Either way, he knew waiting until Monday was his only recourse.

When Monday morning finally rolled around, McMasters discovered that his whole left arm was now brown after getting out of bed. He wanted to scream, but could only gasp, "Oh, my God," as tears welled up in his eyes.

McMasters felt sick in the pit of his stomach. So much so, that he wanted to vomit. Somehow, he was able to suppress doing so. Once again, he quietly dressed, ate breakfast and headed towards Doctor Wentworth's office. This time when he dressed, he put on his riding gloves to cover his now brown left hand.

"So how are you this fine morning?" Wentworth asked.

Without saying a word, McMasters removed his coat and took off his shirt. "Does this answer your question?" he asked as a response.

"Oh, my God," Wentworth gasped. "It has spread."

"Obviously," McMasters snapped. "What can we do about it? How can you cure me, Doc?"

Wentworth looked at McMasters arm very closely. "I don't rightfully know," he admitted. "I ain't found a thing in the medical journals for anything like this. I'll keep looking to see if there is a remedy. Can you come back next week?"

"Do I really have a choice?" McMasters asked.

"I'll try to contact my medical colleagues," Wentworth added. "I will be discrete when I ask."

"Please do, Doc," McMasters pleaded. "I don't want it to spread anymore and I'm beginning to get desperate."

"I'll do what I can," Wentworth responded. "Try not to be concerned."

"I'm already getting concerned, Doc," McMasters confessed. "I am starting to get worried."

Wentworth nodded in acknowledgement. "I'll do what I can," he stated.

McMaster quietly nodded, then left for home. He had a lot to think about as he was living in quiet desperation on what to do next.

The week-long wait proved to be long, tedious and almost overwhelming for McMasters. To make matters worse the brown spot had spread to half his body and the nightmares involving Taurean LeDeau had returned with a vengeance.

So, now he was horrified at the prospects of his skin changing color on top of being totally exhausted.

By the time Monday finally came around, he struggled to get out of bed. Once up, he soon discovered that the brown spot had spread even further. Now his entire body, except for his face and neck, were covered.

McMasters cried out in anguish and despair. He was terribly sick inside as his heart sank and he doubled over in mental and emotional pain.

McMasters hoped that he could do his best to keep his skin condition hidden. He quietly prayed to himself in the hope that Doc Wentworth found a cure for his current condition.

After several minutes of dealing with his own personal terror, McMasters dressed, ate breakfast and then quickly headed into town. Desperation made him ride his horse into town like a cavalry charge in in the war.

When he entered Doc Wentworth's office, he found him reclined in his chair with his feet on his desk and a lit cigar in his hand.

"Doc?" McMasters called out. "Doc?"

Wentworth did not answer. He did not even move.

McMasters began to get concerned as he looked closer. He could see Doc Wentworth had about four inches of ash on the end of cigar that was close to burning his hand. Fear filled the pit of McMasters' stomach. When he went over and touched Wentworth's shoulder, his head slumped downward, and the cigar ash fell in his lap.

McMasters knew immediately that Wentworth was dead. He figures that Wentworth must have lit a cigar then most likely just died while he nodded off.

"Oh, God," McMasters muttered, tears welling up in his eyes.

McMasters knew that he had to contact the sheriff and the undertaker about finding Doc Wentworth dead. Fortunately for him, the sheriff did not ask him many questions or why he was seeing Wentworth. The sheriff knew McMasters' reputation and did not question him about it, figuring that it was natural causes. The only thing McMasters admitted to was that he was seeing Wentworth for a nagging ailment. The sheriff did not bother to approach the subject of what it was exactly, which was just fine with McMasters.

Once McMasters finished talking with the sheriff, he was lost in his thoughts. As he walked his horse out of town, he ignored the usual greetings of some of his friends and neighbors.

"What's wrong with the colonel?" one young lady

asked.

"He found his friend Doc Wentworth dead," the sheriff responded. "He was pretty upset about it."

"Oh, dear," the woman gasped.

After a couple of hundred yards, McMasters mounted his horse. He was now more depressed than ever. At the moment he was uncertain about his future and what exactly to do.

As he slowly rode back home, McMasters thought about finding another voodoo priest, priestess, or some other practitioner in the nearby Louisiana Bayou somewhere. The problem with that idea was they would view his visit as either a great sign of weakness and desperation or that he was planning on leading his men in some form of retaliation against them for his current condition.

Either way, McMasters knew he was in a tough spot.

As futile as it was, he decided to visit one of them. It was his last recourse. He was at his wit's end and it was all that he could do. At this point he was desperate.

One name that popped in his head was Mama Rosa. She had been a rumored local Creole voodoo practitioner that he had heard about. She had helped people medically that were desperate with astonishing success. He wondered if she could help him. McMasters knew that she lived nearby and would not fear him. He dreaded going to see her but knew that he must.

McMasters made his way down the trail that led off the road towards her place. The trail was long and meandering. The further he went, the denser and darker the woods became. The path itself became much thinner as he neared the bayou. At one point, he had to dismount his horse and lead him by the reins. McMasters was filled with apprehension the closer he came to Mama Rosa's place.

As McMasters continued, he heard less and less bird and animal noises. Soon there was total silence, except for his and his horse's footfalls. After several minutes, the path opened up to a clearing that led to the bayou. He saw a small shack that sat on a hill several yards from the swamp.

McMasters was greeted by the sight of a petite, mature somewhat attractive-looking black woman with graying hair sitting in front of her place in a rocking chair. She stared at McMaster, as if she was looking through his soul.

"Colonel McMasters," Mama Rosa said in her Creole accent.

McMasters momentarily stopped in his tracks. "Mama Rosa," he replied.

"You are here for my help," Mama Rosa stated. "You are a desperate man."

McMasters was taken aback. "You know?' he asked. "How?"

"Why else would you be here?' Mama Rosa asked. "But there is nothing I can do for you. Taurean placed a curse on you and his magic is strong."

"You know?" McMasters asked, tying his horse's reins to a nearby tree branch.

"Yes," Mama Rosa responded. "We all know. It is no secret in our world."

McMasters walked towards her. "How?" he asked, perplexed.

"We have our ways," Mama Rosa replied with large smile. "It is something that you have no knowing of. We have our ways."

McMasters took a deep breath and exhaled. "I have a lot of money," he explained. "In fact, I even have some Yankee gold. I will give it to you if you can help me."

"Your gold and money are meaningless, Colonel," Mama Rosa snapped. "There are things in this world more powerful than money. There are forces beyond your understanding. I cannot help you, Colonel."

"I could have your shack burned and you run out of the area," McMasters threatened.

"Aahhh, that you could, Colonel," Mama Rosa calmly replied. "But you will not. Even if you did, it would not help you. You cannot battle what you do not understand."

McMasters was scared, angry and frustrated. Worst of all, he knew that she knew and felt it.

"You can't help me, or you won't?" he asked.

"Even if I could, I would not," Mama Rosa responded. "There are things beyond my control. Good day to you, Colonel."

Mama Rosa stood up, turned around and went into her shack. McMasters felt like a student that had been dismissed in school.

"Wait," McMasters pleaded, but Mama Rosa was already gone.

He thought about following her into her shack but decided against it. A cold chill then ran up his spine. He quickly decided to leave. McMasters knew he was not really wanted there and felt it was better to leave as quickly as possible. He then untied his horse and headed for home. He was now totally at a loss about what to do now.

Once home, McMasters took a nap. He had no energy left. The day had already been draining. After dinner, he went over to his wife Hannah's portrait. "Well, old girl, I don't know what to do," he confessed. "I'm sorry but maybe death…no I don't want that. It's not the answer. Goodnight, my love."

McMasters then headed upstairs to bed. He was mentally, emotionally, and physically exhausted.

Once in bed and asleep, McMasters' nightmares returned with a vengeance. He tossed and turned as the nightmares bedeviled him throughout the night, each one getting progressively worse.

Once again, he woke up in the wee hours of the morning screaming. "Oh, dear God," he sobbed. "I can't take much more of this."

After a few minutes he was able to go back to sleep.

When McMasters finally woke up, his sheets were sweat-logged, his body ached all over and his head hurt. Every muscle in his body creaked in protest to his climbing out of bed. He walked over to his mirror with his eyes not even half open. Once he was able to fully open them, McMasters was shocked and horrified at what he saw.

McMasters was looking in the mirror and seeing Taurean LeDeau looking back at him. He was covered from head to toe with the color of the brown mark that had once been on his arm. Even his hair had changed. Sometime during the night his head and neck had changed color. He looked almost like Taurean LeDeau.

"Oh, God, no!" McMasters screamed in horror.

For all intents and purposes, he had become what he hated.

He had become what Taurean LeDeau warned him about.

A black man.

McMasters dropped to his knees, sobbing uncontrollably. He had never felt so helpless in his whole life. He hadn't felt this sad since the surrender at Appomattox.

Now he felt helpless and lost.

And desperate.

McMasters had to think. What could he do? So far, he had covered up everything except his neck and face. Now, he had to cover them as well.

This was the only option he had left.

McMasters decided to cover most of his face with a

handkerchief and a party mask to cover the area around his eyes. He would tell his housekeeper that it had been Doc Wentworth's orders before he had died on how to treat this skin condition that he had.

When he finally washed up, dressed and completely covered himself, he called down to his housekeeper from the top of the stairs. "Mrs. Ledbetter? Mrs. Ledbetter?"

"Yes," Mrs. Ledbetter responded from the bottom of the stairway. "Is everything alright?"

"Yes," he replied. "Due to a condition of the skin, Doc Wentworth had me covered from head to toe. I don't mean to be an inconvenience, but I will need to take my meals up here for the time being."

"Oh, my," Mrs. Ledbetter gasped. "Are you going to be alright, Colonel?"

"I hope so," McMasters replied. "Please just leave my meals on the table outside of my room."

"Yes, Colonel," Mrs. Ledbetter said with some hesitancy and uncertainty in her voice. "Will there be anything else?"

"Yes," McMasters continued. "If I pay you extra, will you please go to market for me? I also need you to let Mr. Wainright know to stop by for instructions on what to do at the mercantile business. I would also appreciate it if you told people that I do not want any visitors at this time."

"Yes, Colonel," she replied before returning to her duties.

For a few weeks, McMasters was able to stay hidden away from his housekeeper and the stable boy. He only ventured out when absolutely necessary. Then when a heatwave hit, putting Louisiana in temperatures above the mid-nineties, where the humidity was as overwhelming as the heat, he could no longer take being covered up all of the time.

McMasters was getting light-headed and dizzy form

the fiercely hot temperatures and sticky, wet humidity. There wasn't even a respite at night. The hot, sticky air made sleeping futile and uncomfortable.

One evening, while trying to get some relief from the suffocating heat, McMasters ventured out on the balcony off his bedroom. It was all he could do from passing out from the heat. As he stood trying to cool himself off in a faint evening breeze, he was spotted by his stable boy Dean Frederickson, who happened to be staying late cleaning the stable.

Frederickson thought there was something wrong. Colonel McMasters would never let some negro in his house, let alone his bedroom. The only time he did was when it was the help. The problem was, the help had been freed at the end of the war.

Frederickson feared that this nigger had done something terrible to the colonel and started living in his house, and that was the real reason that he had remained covered-up from head to toe these last few weeks.

Frederickson made sure that he told Mrs. Ledbetter and the colonel's associates in the Klan. They would put a stop to this "uppity, trouble-making negro" that was desecrating the colonel's home. When informed of this, Mrs. Ledbetter told him that she had her suspicions about the matter and the colonel's behavior.

The next morning McMasters woke up to a silent, empty house. After dressing and covering himself up he went to get his breakfast tray, but there was nothing outside his room on the table.

"Mrs. Ledbetter?" he called out. "Mrs. Ledbetter?"

There was no answer. Nothing. Only silence.

Dead silence.

McMasters sensed there was something wrong. He initially thought that his housekeeper had succumbed to the heat. Fearing this, he walked cautiously through his home looking for her. After several minutes of searching, he realized that she was not there.

There was no sign of her anywhere.

Mrs. Ledbetter had not shown up at all. He was greatly troubled by this. When he went out to find Frederickson in the stable, there was no sign of his stable boy or his horse Alexander.

"Where could they be?" he asked himself.

McMasters decided to go back into his home and stay hidden. He was hungry and needed to scrounge something up in the kitchen. After finding some salt pork and bread, he retreated back to his bedroom.

After eating he needed to lie down. The overwhelmingly stifling heat was taking its toll on him. After a few minutes of lying in bed thinking, he realized that maybe, just maybe, his housekeeper and his stable boy had discovered his secret. He then wondered if they did not believe it was really him. He was terrified at this prospect.

McMasters was filled with panic. His desperation and fear were almost too much to handle. This overwhelming terror, coupled with the scorching heat and the suffocating humidity, were too much for him and he collapsed on the floor, unconscious. He was on the floor for several hours before recovering. It was almost dusk when he was able to get to his feet.

Upon waking up, he remembered what he had thought before passing out. He knew it was only a matter of time before the Klan showed up. He knew these men and had led them so he knew what was in store for him, should he be found there in this condition.

McMasters knew that he had to flee and possibly hide somewhere.

He began to grab any valuables that he could carry. McMasters made sure that he grabbed all of his money that he had stashed in his house as well as changes of clothing.

After he finished packing, he heard the sound of a lot of horses approaching his home. A short time later he heard the front door being violently opened.

McMasters quickly made sure he was totally covered up. When he opened the door to his room, he was greeted by a half dozen men pointing pistols and rifles at him.

"Howdy boys, what brings you all here?" he asked.

"Colonel McMasters, I presume," his second in command, Jesse Devereaux said, standing directly in front of him.

"Yeah, boys," McMasters replied. "Doc Wentworth said I had some condition of the skin before he died. So, I have to remain all covered up."

"Sure, he did," Deveraux muttered, his voice dripping with skepticism. "How do we know you didn't kill him?"

"No, Jesse, I found him dead," McMasters explained. "That's the God's honest truth."

"Colonel, I must insist that you take off your mask," Devereaux said.

"I'm afraid I cannot do that," McMasters replied. "Doc's orders."

"Doc Wentworth is dead," Devereaux snapped, as he then ripped the mask and handkerchief from McMasters' face, revealing his new skin color. The men stood silently shocked. "You're in a heap of trouble, boy."

"But I am Colonel William McMasters!" McMasters pleaded. "I was being treated by Doc Wentworth for it. I developed this condition that changed the color of my skin. I really did. I'm really not a nigger! My skin changed color somehow!"

"Now boy, I might have been born at night, but it wasn't *last* night," Devereaux barked.

Some of the others noticed that he had some bags

packed in his bedroom.

"It looks like he's planning to steal the colonel's valuables too," Klansman Buford Powell announced.

"But I really am McMasters!" McMasters protested. "Somehow my skin changed. I think Taurean LaDeau put a curse on me."

"Listen boy, you may sound like the colonel, but you ain't him," Devereaux snapped.

"But I am!' McMasters pleaded. "I am. I went to the Virginia Military Institute. I married Hannah Jenkins. I…"

"Shut up!" Devereaux shouted.

"Let's just string this nigger up and be done with it," one of the Klansmen named Fred Hastings barked.

"Don't be hasty, Fred," Devereaux said. "You tell us what you did with the colonel, we may let you live. Or at least give you a sporting chance to get away from us."

"But I *am* the colonel," McMasters cried, with tears running down his cheeks. "I am Colonel McMasters."

Devereaux then punched McMasters in the mouth, drawing blood. "I've had enough of your insolence boy!" he roared. "Let's hang him, boys."

"No, please, no!" McMasters begged. "Please, God, no!"

McMasters begged and pleaded for his life as the Klansmen led him to the field with the tree where Taurean LeDeau was hanged. All his begging and pleading fell on deaf ears.

"Please don't do this!" McMasters cried. "I am Colonel McMasters! I really am!"

Some Klansmen bound his hands behind him and stuffed a gag in his mouth to shut him up. They then placed him atop a horse. Tears welled up in McMasters eyes as he silently prayed for some kind of deliverance. He now knew what Taurean LeDeau had gone through.

A Klansman placed the noose around his neck,

tightening it just enough to effectively do its job. All he could do was sob and shake his head.

A minute later Devereaux gave the order and he was hanged. Immediately afterward he was shot in the head with a Winchester rifle.

As soon as McMasters was dead, his skin immediately changed back to its original color.

"Look!" one Klansman shouted.

The rest of the Klansmen stood around in shock and horror, seeing the body of Colonel William McMasters hanging from a noose, gently swaying back and forth.

"My God, what have we done?" Devereaux gasped in horror.

All the Klansmen stood staring in shock and disbelief at the hanging body of Colonel McMasters, a man who died the way he lived.

With hate.

A Very Fine Specimen

The keepers say I am a very fine specimen. I am lean, with sinewy muscle, and a healthy male in my species. Some may view me as an apex predator. Other predators view me as competition. However, like them we are all another predator's prey.

I don't know how long I've been here. I have lost track of time. It's been at least five years, it must be.

The first year was tough. I tried repeatedly to escape, but to no avail. As the first year became the second and then the third my escape attempts became fewer and far between. By the time the fourth year came, there was really no point. Since then, I pretty much accepted my fate.

I know there isn't much I can do.

Besides, I am a creature of habit. The keepers can detect when I do something out of the ordinary.

I guess the time isn't really important. My survival and well being are.

I am an exhibit in a zoo. I have to admit I am treated well here. My keepers take good care of me. My diet is carefully regulated. I get annual physicals, exams, dental visits and shots as needed. The temperature in my enclosure is regulated to my liking to keep me comfortable. I also get exercise daily.

I really have no complaints about being here, except that I wish I was free.

Well, that's not really true. At least about the complaints. I would like to see my family again and know they are all right.

My family consisted of my parents, two brothers and two sisters. I haven't seen them since we were captured when we were roaming around wild and free. After we were caught, we were separated. I haven't seen them in quite a while. I don't even know if they are dead or alive.

The day we were captured is still fresh in my mind. I remember it like it was yesterday. We were out really doing nothing at the time, except roaming around, enjoying the nice warm weather. Other than that, we were just being a family. We had stopped to rest when, the next thing we knew, we had somehow been trapped. I knew my parents tried to resist as the rest of us attempted to flee. My brothers and I spread out and headed in different directions while my sisters stayed together and bunched up. They were caught first. I was the last one caught. I saw them all tranquilized and captured. That was our last time together as a family, and we were all sent our separate ways.

I can only hope they are in a place like this. They may not like or appreciate it, but they would be safe. Being an exhibit in a zoo isn't all bad. Like I said, we're treated well here. Taken care of, fed regularly and treated medically.

True we have to put up with visitors from time to time, and they're imitating us or calling out to us, but I know it could be far worse for me.

Far worse.

I could be in some kind of circus, expected to perform and do some stupid tricks. If not, I would be punished, or put to use doing some hard labor there. I could be privately owned which might be better than a circus, but that might depend on the owner and what they wanted to do to me. Or, worse yet, I could be used for medical experimentation which would be the cruelest of fates. The thought of that is terrifying.

I just hope my family isn't in one of them.

For a while I had to share my enclosure with an older male. He was not too bad. He spent the bulk of his time sleeping, eating and walking around. He was really too old to do anything and was not a threat to my own safety. It was nice having one of my own species around even if it wasn't for very long. It seemed as if he were just waiting to live out his remaining days quietly, and then simply die.

Then one day his heart stopped. He went peacefully in his sleep. He seemed to welcome it. In the end, he was finally free of this place. Death had been his escape.

From time to time I do think about escaping, but then I decide not to, remembering my previous lessons from before. Besides, I'm too far away from home…I have no idea where to go or how I would even *get* home.

I have no idea where home is anymore.

It's kind of sad how apex predators like my kind are no longer the dominant ones. Now, we are cared for, fed and are basically little more than 'wild' pets or exhibits. All of us, regardless of species and our sizes and strengths, have compromised with that fact. Then again, we all had to.

There was no choice.

We were subdued and captured by an even more dominant and smart apex predator.

But, like I've said earlier, I am alive and living my life. That beats being a dead trophy stuffed and mounted somewhere.

Since I've been here, and for more than a number of times a year, females are brought in for me to mate with. In five years, I think more than twenty of them. Some were more receptive and friendlier than others. Some, while hesitant, eventually gave in to it. I think the keepers got the desired results they were looking for since the females were kept around until they were all impregnated.

The first time I that I was expected to mate, I was hesitant and unsure of myself. But they let me have my way with them as much as I wanted for as long as I wanted. That was quite nice. But best of all was the companionship. I wasn't alone.

I know I have several offspring, both male and female out there. Where they're at or how they are I don't know. Then again, I wasn't supposed to. I imagine they were sent off to other places like this.

Sometimes I wonder if that's what my siblings are doing as well. Are my brothers to act as studs to females so they can breed some more and my sisters are sent off to be impregnated by other males for the same purpose?

While there is little I could do about it, I hope not.

At least my cage (or should I say my enclosure, because there are no physical bars holding me in) is fairly nice. There's plenty of open area in which to roam, a decent shelter and all of the similar comforts of my real home. The entire enclosure's surroundings are eerily reflective of where I used to live all my free life.

While there are no bars or fences of sorts keeping me in, there are towering walls equipped with electrical wiring that generates extremely uncomfortable but non-fatal charges. I've experienced them, while trying to escape a couple of times, when I was first here.

I know there are other animals around. I've seen them. From certain vantage points in my enclosure I can see bears, apes, and white-tailed deer.

The bears are very interesting. At times they are real characters. They seem happy and content enough and almost willing to do anything for food. Sometimes we look at each other for great lengths of time. I just wonder if we thought about similar things, like about being free.

I felt some sympathy for one poor old bear. I don't know how long he was here, but it was much longer than if he had lived in the wild. He became old and ill, and had to be put to sleep.

At least the keepers were gentle and humane about it.

Still it was kind of sad not seeing him out there frolicking in the sun and care-free. I had grown used to seeing him every day.

Now he's gone.

I liked him way better than the monkeys.

Also, nearby are the apes. This includes the gorillas, chimpanzees and others in the primate species. Whoever said they were directly related to men had to have been insane. On one hand they are right, especially in the fact that they care for their young and are social animals. On the other hand, I wonder. They are covered in hair and smell a lot worse. Besides, they act a lot dumber.

I observed some monkeys…well chimpanzees I think…run around and act stupid, throwing poop at each other. Besides, they aren't very nice. On top of that they always seem to be fussing and fighting over something. I wish the keepers hadn't put them so close. Some days I can smell them, and it is not good.

At least the gorillas don't do that. They act stoic and pretty much keep to themselves.

As for the deer nearby, they pretty much stay quiet and uninteresting. They are curious, and we watch each other but that's about it. They just roam around peacefully, not bothering anybody. I wish at times I could eat one, but that is not happening. At least not here.

We're in a zoo and deer are not on the menu here.

Still, all in all, they are nice to watch and observe. They aren't as bothersome as the monkeys, nor do they stink like them.

My typical day is basically waking up, eating, roaming

around my enclosure…sometimes I run around it, take a nap, roam around some more, eat again, then relax and watch the stars at night and wonder all kinds of random thoughts.

When females were provided you could add sex to my routine. Sometimes it was a couple of times of day or more. Not every day or all of the time, but enough. Certain times of the year and on a lot of days that was all we did. Other than eating and sleeping, there wasn't a whole lot more to do than that.

I heard the keepers talking a while ago. I know I'll be provided with female companionship soon. Plus, they told me directly. I may not be able to understand everything they say, but I understood that.

From what I could figure out, when there was only one of a certain species and it didn't have companionship then it became depressed, and its life expectancy was shorter.

I guess that was true for most of the species of animals here.

It makes sense. Many animals have a kind of social need for others of their species.

Whether it was with one of the females that I mated with before or another one I have never met, I don't know. I do wonder if this female has had other offspring or was saved for just this special occasion. I realize that's why I was thoroughly cleaned earlier, so that I look my best.

Hopefully the keepers took the time to make sure we were compatible. I assume they probably have done so. I guess they do care about me to do that. They do treat me well and we've built up a kind of trust of sorts, especially since I no longer try to escape.

I'm not aggressive anymore around them either. When I used to be, I was always quickly sedated.

Don't get me wrong, I'm not totally complacent. I still long to be free. Every once in a while, I do show a temper and bare my fangs. It lets them know when I'm not pleased. But that isn't very often.

Even though this is my home now, I still haven't gotten totally used to the place. I know that I am watched and monitored most of the time, and this usually includes sex and most other bodily functions.

I know I'm watched when I sleep. Especially when there's a female present. That's a given. It's probably to see how we interact when resting or sleeping.

For the keepers, my life is almost clinical in everything I do. That is how much I am studied and observed. It involves eating habits, sleeping habits, mating habits, all activities and even grooming habits. It goes on and on.

For now, I'll take a walk in the wooded area of the enclosure. It's peaceful and relaxing there. It reminds me of home. It's similar to the area where my family and I were captured. It has all the familiar trees and foliage, the same tall grass, a flowing stream, wildflowers and even a tremendously large stone that's flat on the top where I sit and rest upon several times each day.

It's very scenic, and I like it here. It's my favorite part of the enclosure. I know most of the females I mated with like it, too.

Like life, some days are better than others. Most days I am pretty happy and content. Very few others I am not. Mostly because of the loneliness here.

Because of that, some days I have trouble deciding what to do.

I imagine getting a companion will change that. We will be spending almost every waking hour together or near each other.

I figure we will get acquainted first, and depending on

the female it might take a little while. I may offer my food to her as a kind of welcoming friendly gesture. This, I hope, will be regarded in the right way. Then if we are really compatible, we will eventually mate. If that happens, and we have offspring, I wonder if we'll be allowed to keep them this time. I know they let some species keep their offspring out of necessity. It would be nice if they did the same.

I hear my keepers approaching. I'd better be ready and greet them like I usually do. Apparently, they are finally bringing my companion. I have to admit I am more than a little curious, excited and even concerned.

Hopefully we are compatible. I would hate to end up with a companion that I would fight with.

The keepers are now moving me to an area of the enclosure where I can see, but where I am not too close. They do not want me to frighten the female or make her uncomfortable by appearing too aggressive upon our meeting.

From what I can tell they want us to be introduced slowly and gradually to each other. I think it's to make sure we get along and for our own safety.

That is understandable.

So, for now I'll just wait until told to move forward.

Here come the keepers. There are two in front, four that are around my new female companion who are partially obstructing my view of her and two in back of her.

I watch with growing anticipation and uncertainty as they enter my enclosure. I have backed up a couple of steps to show I'm not aggressive.

Finally, I am able to see the female of my species. Physically, she's a very fine specimen…the finest I've seen and encountered so far. She's sleek, with fine lines and curves, while her hair and body have a nice sheen to them.

She's seen me and is looking over at me curiously. I don't sense any apprehension from her in any way. That is good.

The keepers are slowly leading me over towards her. As I get nearer to her, she's even more impressive up close and it seems she's looking at me the same way that I am at her. We both notice that the keepers are slowly backing away to see what happens next.

It became a kind of friendly, non-aggressive stand-off, with us just staring.

I have decided to end this by giving the female some of my food. She has taken it and begun to eat. She seems to have accepted my gesture of friendship and possible kinship.

The female is slowly approaching me and sniffing. She has a fragrance to her that is very welcoming and nice. The female is leaning into my body, touching me, and trusting me.

I think we're compatible. Slowly the keepers are exiting our enclosure. I think they know or believe we're compatible as well. They should be happy with this. Two very fine specimens of our species, compatible and finally put together in a single enclosure.

After a few hours of getting better acquainted and sitting side-by-side, the keepers returned. At first, we were filled with great fear and apprehension because we both thought they were going to take one of us away or separate us again.

The keepers went about their business, only occasionally keeping a wary eye on us. We noticed they were erecting a sign, and after its completion they departed. We know they would return soon to feed us again.

We both headed over to check out their handiwork. We stood there reading the sign that read in several different languages we weren't familiar with, including one in English: Earthlings - Male & Female: Homo sapiens.

She leans her head on my shoulder, totally comfortable with me, as I put my arm around her to try and be reassuring. I can tell we both need each other. I still cannot get over how beautiful and friendly she is. I can hardly wait for us to make love. Right now, it's just nice being next to her.

It truly has been an eventful day. We both gained much wanted and needed companionship today. We will continue to get acquainted and to know each other better, get some much-needed sleep and live our future together.

We are just two very fine specimens, a very long way from home and dreaming of freedom.

About the author

Tom Sawyer is a Michigan writer. Since starting out as a 17-year-old with a weekly newspaper, he has authored the novels *The Lighthouse, Fire Sale, The Sisigwad Papers, the Last Big Hit*, the *Dracula* sequel *Shadows in the Dark*, the acclaimed collection *Dark Harbors,* then *From Paradise to Hell,* followed by the chilling novel *White Out* and the science fiction collection *The Thing From Uranus*. He has also written a number of short stories that have been featured in various publications. A lifelong Waterford resident, he and his wife Colleen have three children.

www.blackbedsheetbooks.com

www.blackbedsheetbooks.com

Made in the USA
Columbia, SC
10 March 2023

13508797R00133